NOEL

A novella

TERRY TOLER

Noel
Published by: BeHoldings, LLC

Copyright ©2024, **BeHoldings, LLC**
Terry Toler
All Rights Reserved

Book Cover: BeHoldings Publishing
Editor: Jeanne Leach
Contributing Editor: Donna Toler

For information email: terry@terrytoler.com.

Our books can be purchased in bulk for promotional, educational, and business use. Please contact your bookseller or the BeHoldings Publishing Sales department at: sales@terrytoler.com

For booking information email: booking@terrytoler.com.
First U.S. Edition: September, 2024
Printed in the United States of America
ISBN 978-1-954710-24-5

OTHER BOOKS BY TERRY TOLER

Fiction

Save The Girls

The Ingenue

Saving Sara

Save The Queen

No Girl Left Behind

The Launch

Body Count

Save Me Twice

Powerful Enemies

Deadly Games

Don't Be Careful

Wintervention

Saving Alex

Forsaken

Fugitives

Cliff Hangers: Anna

Cliff Hangers: Mr. & Mrs. Platt

Cliff Hangers: The Quarterback

Cliff Hangers: Macy

Cliff Hangers: Not, Not Guilty

The Blue Rose

Triggers

Seven Year Rich

Noel

The Book Club

The Book Club Murder

The Book Club Rescue

The Longest Day

The Reformation of Mars

The Late, Great Planet Jupiter

The Great Wall of Ven-Us
Saturn: The Eden Experiment
The Mercury Protocols
The Heart of Pluto

Non-Fiction

How to Make More Than a Million Dollars
The Heart Attacked
Seven Years of Promise
Mission Possible
Marriage Made in Heaven
21 Days to Physical Healing
21 Days to Spiritual Fitness
21 Days to Divine Health
21 Days to a Great Marriage
21 Days to Financial Freedom
21 Days to Sharing Your Faith
21 Days to Mission Possible
7 Days to Emotional Freedom
Uncommon Finances
Uncommon Health
Uncommon Marriage
The Jesus Diet
Suddenly Free
Feeling Free

For more information on these books and other resources visit
terrytoler.com.

1

New York City

"What made you get into acting, Noel?" Char asked me. Char Kelly was an agent to the stars. Confirmed by the wall of autographed photos of famous movie stars to my right.

"I've had the acting bug since I was a teenager," I replied. "I was in a few plays in high school and fell in love with it."

"How did you get into the academy?"

I shrugged. I wasn't sure how. A little over a year ago, I packed my bags and moved to New York from Philadelphia. Impulsively. To take a year of acting lessons at the New York Academy of Acting. NYAA. Even though I graduated and was told I could make a career out of it, the dream still seemed impossible.

"All I did was send in an application and a demo tape," I said. "I was shocked when I got the call that I was accepted."

"Did you know someone who helped you get in?"

Apparently, Char was surprised as well.

What am I doing here? I'm as out of place as a toaster in a bathtub.

"No. I sent in the application cold turkey. I guess someone liked my look."

Char furrowed her brow. She either had a good plastic surgeon or was aging naturally because her bigger than average lips moved easily, and only a few wrinkles were visible. I knew her to be fifty-five from my pre-interview research, but she didn't look a day over forty. Her professionally coiffed hair, perfectly manicured nails, and designer clothes made me feel self-conscious since her shoes probably cost more than my entire wardrobe.

"I'm impressed," Char said. "Only five percent of applicants make it in. Half of those can't cut it."

"I'm a hard worker."

"Of the half who do somehow manage to last the year and graduate, only one percent go on to make it big. Acting is a tough business."

"I'm a tough girl, Ms. Kelly."

"Good answer."

Char obviously didn't get to her position without being tough either. CEO of one of the largest agencies in the world in a male-dominated industry. The office was on the fifteenth floor of a high-rise office building in downtown Manhattan. I also learned from my research that she had more than a dozen agents working for her and a support staff of a hundred.

"Please call me Char."

I was told by a fellow student that Char was short for Chardonnay, but I hadn't been able to confirm that information and certainly wasn't going to ask.

"Please call me Noel," I said, then mentally kicked myself since she had called me Noel seconds before.

She smiled at my gaffe which should've relaxed my angst but didn't.

"Janice is a good friend of mine," she said.

Dr. Janice McKinney was one of my teachers and my academic advisor. For whatever reason, she liked me and had set up the interview with Char.

"She says you have potential," Char added. "I've never seen her so effusive about a student."

"I love Dr. McKinney. I'm honored that she gave me such a glowing recommendation."

"You should be. She doesn't give out compliments easily."

"Don't I know it."

"I noticed that you're married," Char said. "Are you planning on having kids anytime soon? That could make a difference if we're shopping you for a movie role."

She obviously saw the wedding rings on my finger. How could she miss them? I kept twirling them around on my finger. A nervous habit.

"Actually, my husband passed away a couple years ago."

"Oh. I'm sorry to hear that. I didn't know."

"It's okay. I still wear my rings. I haven't been able to take them off."

"How long were you married?"

"One day."

Her eyebrows raised. "I'm so sorry. You're so young to suffer such loss."

"I'm twenty-one."

"How did he die?"

Char changed the subject before I could answer.

"Believe it or not, twenty-one is old in terms of starting an acting career," she said.

"That's what Dr. McKinney said. Early on, she tried to discourage me. I thought she was even trying to make me quit."

"She wanted to see if you have what it takes. She's only hard on the ones with potential."

"I think I do have potential."

Dr. McKinney had coached me to be confident but not egotistical. I think I'd found the right balance. Char exuded all kinds of confidence. I wanted to be more like her.

She looked up and down at me. Sizing me up. Something she did several times since the interview started.

"A world-class cellist doesn't start learning how to play the cello at age twenty," she said in a slightly condescending teacher-voice. "You're behind the learning curve."

Does this mean she isn't going to take me? Because I don't have enough experience?

"I realize the odds are stacked against me."

Tears welled up inside me. I fought them back. Mostly because I felt a rejection coming on. As improbable as getting into the academy had been, being represented by the foremost agent in the business was only a pipe dream.

It also may have been because she brought up Chris. The emotions were still raw, even two years later. I blamed Dr. McKinney for that. She wouldn't let me move on from them. She taught me to think of my husband when I acted out an emotional scene. To draw upon my grief and anger.

I wasn't sure if that was good for me or not. It probably made me a better actress, but it wreaked havoc on my emotional well-being.

"I'd like to represent you," she said unexpectedly.

I had leaned forward and almost fell out of my chair. My heart skipped a beat from the sudden rush of jubilation.

"I like you. I like your look. I like your spunkiness. You've suffered a loss and overcame it."

"It's made me who I am today."

"Janice has sent me a half dozen people over the years. Not very many, considering the hundreds who've graduated from that place. I've made a lot of money off her referrals. I would never turn down someone she refers to me. She might not send anymore."

She's going to represent me!

I could hardly believe the words coming out of her mouth. Her client list was a who's who in the movie industry. Dr. McKinney said Char could open doors I could never open on my own. I had no idea why she would bother with someone like me. I was a nobody. As insecure as a toy poodle in a room full of Rottweilers. Filled with more self-doubt than I started the academy with.

Still, I could barely contain my excitement. "Thank you for believing in me. It means a lot to me."

Then I remembered something. An unanswered question that hung over the room like a San Francisco fog.

How did my husband die?

2

Did she still want me to answer the question? My husband's death was something I avoided talking about. I took a deep breath. For whatever reason, I wanted to tell her.

"You asked me how my husband died. Chris and I were high-school sweethearts. He was my first love. My only love. I didn't date anyone before Chris and haven't dated anyone since."

I realized I wasn't answering the question.

"He died in a scuba-diving accident on our honeymoon."

The Cliff's Notes version was my go-to the few times the subject had come up over the two years.

For some reason, I wanted to tell her more. I felt drawn to Char. I genuinely liked her. To the point I felt like I could bare my soul to her. Maybe because she believed in me and wanted to represent me. Maybe because the grief had been pent up for so long, it needed to come out.

"We were married in Philadelphia," I said, since she didn't act like she wanted me to stop. The story began to spill out of my mouth before I could stop it whether she wanted it to or not. "That's where we're from. In a small church off the Main Line. At eleven in the morning. Our reception was at a hotel in Valley Forge."

The words came fast. I had to remind myself to breathe.

Char looked intently at me. It emboldened me to continue even though I wondered if I was sharing too much.

I changed positions in the chair. Crossed my legs so I could lean forward even more. Brushed away the bangs from my eyes then nervously clasped my hands together on my lap.

"After our reception, we rode a limo to the airport and caught a plane to the Bahamas. We checked into our hotel just after midnight. As you can imagine, we were exhausted. We were so tired we fell into bed. We didn't really have a normal wedding night, if you know what I mean."

Char nodded and smiled.

Too much information.

For some reason, I couldn't stop myself.

"Ours is a real love story. While we couldn't wait to be together, we were so tired, we decided to get some sleep and wait until the next day. We made love for the first time the next morning."

She smiled. "That's a beautiful story."

"I'd like to say it was beautiful and romantic. Truthfully, it was awkward. Both of us were nervous and didn't really know what we were doing."

Shut up, Noel. You're rambling.

"Looking back though, it was the most incredible moment of my life."

"Sounds like you really loved him. And miss him ... still." Her words trailed off like the fade on the ending to a song.

I nodded. Not sure if I could complete the next sentence in my head.

"What I wouldn't give to go back in time ... and tell Chris not to get on that boat."

She seemed moved. I could tell because she cleared her throat for the first time. Like she was on the verge of choking up.

Emboldened, I continued with the rest of the story in detail. About how Chris had gotten his dive certificate the week before. I was claustrophobic and had no desire to go underwater. Especially after reading about diving in the Grand Bahamas. The waters were filled with sharks. Hammerheads, lemon sharks, reef sharks, and the aggressive tiger sharks.

"I stayed behind at the resort swimming pool. I still remember how excited I was for Chris when the dive boat left the marina. How excited he was. He waved goodbye to me from the boat. Kept waving until he was out of sight. That's my last memory of him."

"I can only imagine what you were feeling."

"While he was gone, I missed him so much and couldn't wait for him to get back to the resort. I saw the boat returning from a distance away. I was confused when I didn't see Chris. He wasn't on it. It didn't make sense to me."

"That must've been horrible."

"As soon as I saw the dive captain's face and how the others were acting, I knew something was wrong. I panicked. They had already airlifted Chris to the hospital. They rushed me there even though I knew in my heart he was already dead. The rest is kind of a blur."

A tear escaped and rolled down my cheek. I gently brushed it away.

My voice cracked as I continued.

"Something went wrong on the dive. Chris's equipment malfunctioned. They found him unconscious at the bottom of the reef. By then, it was too late. They brought him to the surface and tried to revive him, but they couldn't."

I fought to regain my composure. The last thing I wanted was to fall completely apart in her office.

"Less than twenty-four hours after we left the wedding reception, he was gone," I said, barely above a whisper.

"That's one of the saddest things I've ever heard."

"I know."

I bit my lip to fight back the deluge of tears trying to escape my eyes.

"At first, right after it happened, I was numb. I actually prefer that feeling. It lasted a couple months. Then I got angry. At the dive captain who should've been watching his divers. At the diving buddy who was supposed to stay with Chris. The equipment manufacturer who made the faulty regulator."

"It should never have happened. I'd be furious."

"I was. I sued them."

"How did you get through it?"

"My faith in God helped me."

She nodded making me wonder if she believed in God.

That's not entirely true. My anger eventually turned toward God even though I tried not to cross the line into blaming him. But I had a lot of questions and didn't find any good answers.

Why did you bring us together if I could only be married to him for a day?

Did I miss your will for my life? Was I never supposed to marry Chris to begin with?

If we hadn't married, would he still be alive?

Why did you let this happen?

"It took a long time for me to be at peace with it. Or at least accept the fact I couldn't do anything about it."

"Like you said, it made you who you are today."

"If I had to do it over again, I'd still marry Chris a hundred out of a hundred times. For just that one day together."

That one incredible morning. I'll never forget it as long as I live.

Char dabbled at the side of her eye although she pretended to be adjusting her makeup. She abruptly leaned forward and opened a file in front of her. She took out a document and shoved it across the desk.

"This is my standard representation agreement," she said. "If you'd like me to represent you, I will."

"Of course. I'm thrilled."

She handed me a pen. I didn't even read it. Simply signed on the line and handed it back to her. She signed it and put it back in the file.

"I'll have my assistant make you a copy before you leave. My daughter Rose will be the agent assigned to you."

"Thank you. You won't regret it. I look forward to working with her."

I must be special if she wants her daughter to be my agent.

"Good. What are you doing tomorrow afternoon?"

"Nothing. Why?"

"I have an audition for you."

"Already?"

"Yes. It's a *Love Only* movie."

The *Love Only* channel showed nonstop sappy romance movies. Chris loved them. His idea of a good date was sitting on the couch with popcorn and watching a movie.

"Janice said you wouldn't do nudity or horror films."

I nodded.

"A *Love Only* movie is perfect for you then. You look like a *Love Only* girl to me."

"Do you know anything about the role?"

"It's a Christmas movie. You'll be auditioning for the female lead."

Chris loved their Christmas movies. Christmas in July and the around-the-clock movies that started in November and ran through the holidays were his favorites.

He would flip out if he knew I was about to audition for one.

"And your name is Noel. That might help."

"Do you know who the leading man is?"

"Avery Johnson."

"You're kidding! He's like the biggest star on the channel."

"He's the biggest star on the planet. I wish I represented him."

"Now I'm nervous."

"You'll be fine. Don't be disappointed if they don't pick you for this role. This is your first audition. Nobody gets the first role they audition for. But I want you on their radar. I've been filling roles for them for years. I think they'll like you. Hopefully, they'll pick you for a lesser role to start, and you can go from there."

"I'll take anything."

"That's the spirit. Call me when you're done with the audition."

She handed me her card.

"That's my personal cell phone number."

I stared at it.

A schoolgirl giggle escaped my mouth.

I have an agent.

I have Char Kelly's personal cell phone.

I have an audition.

For a movie.

With Avery Johnson.

My heart was full of joy.

Then I remembered Chris and that he wasn't there to see it.

My heart was sad again.

3

After her mother, Char Kelly, signed Noel Day to a representation agreement, the young, aspiring actress was handed off to Rose to manage. With instructions to get her ready for an audition for a *Love Only* Christmas movie.

In one day!

And why do I always get the newbies?

Rose was as nervous as Noel. The *Love Only* audition was a big deal and a lot was expected of her.

They spent the afternoon taking care of the prerequisites. New headshots and portfolio package. A complete makeover. Hair, makeup, and new clothes for the audition. The photographer was busy, so they didn't finish the shoot until late in the evening.

While they waited, Rose told Noel what to expect.

"Erin Palmer is the Vice President of Casting for Love Only. She's the boss. No one gets a lead role without her approval. We'll get there fifteen minutes before your appointment. When your name is called, you'll go in the room. I'll be there with you. You'll see a table facing a makeshift set. There'll be lights set up. A camera and cameraman. You'll walk directly to your mark. An X will be clearly visible on the floor or carpet. Stand there and face the table."

"Got it."

"Erin Palmer will be sitting behind the table. I'll give her your portfolio and information. Avery Johnson will be there as well."

Noel blinked twice in confusion. "Avery will be there?"

"I'm sure he will. It's part of his contract. He has a say in choosing his leading ladies."

"As if I weren't nervous enough."

Rose went through everything she could think of even though she was sure the academy had taught Noel the basics of an audition.

"It'll be held at the Plaza Hotel. A car will pick us up at twelve-fifteen, but I want you here at eleven, so we have time to refresh your hair and makeup."

"Can I see the script so I can memorize my lines tonight?"

"No. Erin Palmer has a certain way of doing things. She doesn't want a rehearsed audition. She wants to see if you can read the lines on the spot, process them, then turn them into a memorable performance with no practice."

"That's a lot of pressure."

"Wait until you get on the movie set where the production costs are $5000.00 an hour. A bad actor can cost them a fortune."

"Do you at least know anything about the character?"

"I have the casting call info. Come with me."

Rose went to her office and found it in the file on her desk. Noel followed her in and sat down on the chair across from her desk. She read it to her.

"Love Only movie. *That Figures*. Female. Leading. Character is attractive. Between five six and five nine. Under thirty years of age. Excitable and eager. Insecure but willing to stand up for herself if the situation demands it. She's funny. Ability to deliver a humorous line a must."

"Sounds like me."

"Description. Set at Christmas time. A self-taught pastry chef opens a bakery in a small town in middle America."

Noel groaned. "That doesn't sound like me at all. I can't bake to save my life."

"That's why they call it acting."

"I suppose."

"While business is booming, Sarah—"

"Ooh. I like that name."

"Sarah struggles to keep the business afloat. She knows nothing about finances and hires an accountant from a CPA firm. His name is Stephen. With a ph. Not a v."

"Avery Johnson?"

"Right."

"Hence the name of the movie, *That Figures*," Noel said. "Accounting numbers. Clever."

Rose kept reading.

"Stephen falls in love immediately and begins pursuing Sarah. She's attracted to him as well, but her sister is suffering from cancer—"

"Aww."

"Between running the bakery and caring for her sister, Sarah doesn't have time for love."

"She's emotionally conflicted. Her sister is probably encouraging her to choose love, but she feels guilty. Great idea for a story."

"This is a complicated tale where grief and love intersect."

"Been there. Done that. Sounds like my life."

"Rehearsals begin in May. Filming in June. Most *Love Only* movies are shot in fifteen days."

"Wow. That's fast."

"These are lower budget films. Two million or so. Avery makes about half of that."

"A million dollars a picture. That's amazing."

Rose had Noel practice reading some lines. After hearing her a few times, she had to admit the girl was good. Even then, she probably wasn't ready for the big time. But Rose wasn't about to tell her mother the audition was a waste of time. She didn't get to voice her opinions. They'd be summarily dismissed.

Didn't matter. These casting calls were mostly for show. *Love Only* continually said they were looking for new talent and probably were, but Rose knew how the audition would go. They'd call in a couple hundred girls, reject them all, then call one of their old standbys and book them for the part. At least Noel would get some experience out of it. Her mother probably thought she needed it as well.

Rose had worked like a dog at the agency since she could walk, starting in the mail room until she worked her way up to agent. She had graduated from Columbia University with honors while working full time at the agency, yet nothing she did was ever good enough for her mother.

They should make a movie about her life.

The Daughter in the Shadow. A coming-of-age short film about a lonely girl living under the thumb of an emotionally strained mother incapable of uttering one crumb of affirmation to her starving daughter.

Rose smiled at the thought. Hundreds of people in the industry would love to be in her position. That's because they had no idea how hard it was to be the daughter of Char Kelly. Who demanded more of Rose than she did the others in order not to show favoritism.

Rose tried not to let her thoughts show on her face. Noel didn't seem to notice. She was distracted by the whirlwind Rose was putting her through.

The negative thoughts wouldn't go away.

How am I supposed to get ahead in the agency when my mother always gives me the people with no experience?

The fastest way to gain her mother's approval was to fill the coffers with money and prestige. Rose needed a big win to get her mother's attention. That wasn't going to happen until she managed a star. One wouldn't be given to her. A newbie would have to someday hit it big.

Landing the leading role in a *Love Only* movie opposite Avery Johnson would be a good start. It didn't get much bigger than that. That'd be a huge feather in Rose's cap.

Probably not going to happen.

Noel didn't need to get the part, but things needed to go well. So Rose could maintain her place on the lowest rung of the corporate ladder, which for her, was the ladder of her mother's approval.

She was almost resigned to the fact that she'd never fully reach the top of that ladder.

For now, she just needed to get Noel through the audition without embarrassing the agency.

4

The next day

Noel showed up before eleven. On time was a check in her favor. Hair and makeup went quickly. Picking out an outfit took the most time. Rose decided the one they chose the day before was too glamorous.

She'd bolted out of bed in the middle of the night with that realization. At three in the morning, she decided to think outside the box. Reading the casting call the day before had her rethinking her clothing choices.

What would a pastry chef in a small Midwest town wear? Not a dress. Jeans and a tee shirt that could get dirty with flour, sugar, and butter would be the likely choice.

Not high heels. Sneakers or flats. Sarah would be on her feet all day. She'd need something comfortable. Her hair also didn't need to be overly styled. It'd be pulled back in a bun all day.

Risky to dress Noel that way. The audition room would be filled with girls decked out. Noel might be the only one in jeans.

She'll stand out from the others.

Noel didn't object. In fact, she agreed. Another plus in her favor. This girl seemed like she'd be easy to work with on a set.

Rose went with everything except the hair in a bun. Noel had naturally flowing beautiful, dark-brown, shoulder-length hair that fit the image of Sarah in her head.

The driver picked them up on time, and they snuck out without her mother seeing Noel. Rose didn't want her second guessing her decisions. The limo began the approximately twenty-three-minute ride to the Plaza Hotel.

"You know, my mother's name is short for Chardonnay," Rose said. The bar in the limo reminded her of that fact.

"I'd heard that."

"My name is actually pronounced Rosé."

"Really. I didn't know that."

"Yeah. My family is weird. I come from a long line of drinkers. That's why I go by Rose."

Noel didn't respond. She kept staring out the window, clearly deep in thought. Probably getting mentally prepared for the audition.

Rose now felt confident the audition would go off without a major hitch. At least, well enough that it wouldn't reflect negatively on her. Noel was as ready as she was going to be for her first time.

"Remember, Noel," Rose said, "they want you to do well as much as you do."

"I'll do the best I can."

"Do better than that."

"I'll try."

"Own the character," Rose said.

"What does that even mean?"

"I have no idea! But it sounds good."

They both laughed hard, releasing some of the tension in the limo.

They arrived at the registration desk manned by a *Love Only* employee exactly fifteen minutes early. As expected, the hallway to the meeting room was lined with at least a hundred girls. All dressed to the hilt. Rose wondered if she had made the right choice going with the casual look.

Many of the ladies looked bored like they'd done this a million times. Others seemed petrified, like the proverbial deer in headlights. All of them took at least one look at Noel. A few flashed looks of disapproval.

The lady behind the table told them to follow her. She led them into the audition room. Rose was sure some dirty looks were directed at them behind their backs as they got in ahead of the other girls.

"It's nice to work for Char Kelly," Rose muttered to herself.

A thirty-something blonde beauty was standing at the front of the room reading some lines.

The assistant told them to stand a few feet behind the table. Rose leaned over and whispered in Noel's ear. "This'll be good for you to see so you know what to expect."

"She's good," Noel whispered back.

The woman was below average with no shot at getting the part.

Erin Palmer looked back and waved at Rose. Avery Johnson sat next to her with his head down, back to them. He was dressed casually. Jeans and a polo shirt with loafers. Maybe she had made a good choice after all.

"Thank you," Erin said to the woman when she finished overacting the lines. "We'll be in touch if we have a part for you."

The woman scurried for the door and flashed a resigned smile Rose's way. Like she knew she had no chance of getting the role.

Rose waited for Erin to finish typing something in her computer. When she looked back a second time and held out her hand, Rose walked quickly toward her and handed her Noel's portfolio package.

"You're up," Rose said to Noel. "Walk to the mark and kill it."

Noel walked slowly but confidently and took her place in front of the blinding lights on each side and in front of her. She didn't look nervous at all.

The nervousness returned in Rose, effectively eroding her previous confidence.

"State your name, age, and height please, for the camera," Erin said.

"Noel Day. I'm twenty-one. Five foot seven and a half inches tall."

From Rose's vantage point, she could see Noel through the camera lens. She looked good.

Avery was no longer looking down. He was staring at Noel. Rose didn't know if that was a good sign or not.

Erin stood and held out a piece of paper across the table. Noel stepped forward, took it from her and stepped back to her mark.

"When you're ready, read the lines on the front page."

Noel took about thirty seconds to read the lines to herself. When she finished, she looked up at the ceiling, took a deep breath, and began.

"That's it? That's what you want to ask me? What do I want to do today? My sister is in a hospital bed. She might die. And you want to know what I want to do today?"

Noel had the right level of intensity behind the words and had captured the essence of the character immediately.

"Okay. Let's see," Noel said sarcastically. "How about a movie? What do you want to see? I know. Let's go Christmas shopping. How fun. Like I'm in the mood for Christmas."

Noel delivered the last lines with the perfect amount of emotion behind the words and without looking down once at the paper. Impressive that she could memorize them that fast.

"Do you want to know what I want to do today?" Noel continued after a slight hesitation, speaking barely above a whisper. "I want to pick up my sister from the hospital and take *her* to a movie. Take *her* Christmas shopping. Do the things we've done every Christmas for years."

A tear ran down her cheek. She was really into character. This must be what owning the character meant.

"I don't want her to be sick anymore ... I don't want her to suffer. I don't want her ... to ... die."

Wow!

Rose was moved inside.

As fast as it had started, it was over. Noel turned back toward the table and waited for instructions.

Rose couldn't believe how well she did. Much better than in practice.

"Thank you," Erin said. "Please read the lines on the back of the sheet."

Noel turned the sheet over and read through the lines quickly. She looked back at the camera. Her demeanor changed.

"You don't like to do interesting things," she said smiling broadly. "You're an accountant."

Rose saw Avery's shoulders rise and fall, like he was laughing. Erin Palmer was smart to make the girls go from an intense dramatic scene, to delivering a one liner. That had to be extremely difficult to do.

Noel did it effortlessly.

"Thank you, Noel," Erin said. "Good job. Great name for a Christmas movie, by the way."

As Noel started to walk away, Avery Johnson abruptly stood to his feet.

"I'd like to read a few lines with Noel," he said.

Rose's heart started to race.

This had to be a good sign. Avery wouldn't take the time to read with Noel unless he was interested in her for the role.

5

Avery said he wanted to read a few lines with Noel. Rose knew this happened sometimes but had never seen it before at an audition.

Noel stopped walking. She backed up to her mark as Avery stepped out from behind the table. He circled around the camera and walked over and stood next to her. He introduced himself and offered his hand. She shook it.

"That's a good idea, Avery," Erin said. "What do you want to read?"

Rose's hopes were out of control. How she'd love to go back to the office and tell her mother that Noel got the part. She tempered the enthusiasm. Noel wouldn't get the role on the spot. It'd take days for them to make a decision. Maybe even a call back before they finalized things.

Rose could dream. Even a call back would be a win. And good for Noel.

Bring it home, Noel!

She wanted to shout encouragement at the top of her lungs. All she could think to do was cross her fingers behind her back.

Avery Johnson had what looked to be a full script in his hand. He handed Noel the script and told her what he wanted her to do.

"We're going to continue with that same scene," Avery said to Erin. "The one about me being an uninteresting accountant."

Erin rifled through her copy of the script until she found the spot.

"I'm ready," Erin said. "When you are."

"You have the first line," Avery said to Noel. "Take your time."

Noel began immediately. "You don't like to do interesting things," she said, holding the script off to the side, speaking directly to him without looking at it. "You're an accountant. Interesting to you are spreadsheets and the nightly news!"

Rose laughed out loud. So did Erin.

They continued for a few lines. Bantering back and forth. Rose saw real chemistry between them. They looked good together. Avery was movie-star-handsome. Noel was his equal in a girl-next-door kind of way.

It seemed like Erin saw it as well, because she sat forward in her chair, elbows on the table, no longer looking at the script in front of her. Watching them intently.

"Look up," Avery said. Pointing upward.

"It's a mistletoe," Noel said shyly. "If I didn't know any better, I might think you led me here on purpose."

He took a step closer to her.

"And what if I did?" he said coyly.

"Look it's snowing," Noel said, looking up again.

"Don't change the subject," he said, his eyes squarely focused on her face.

Noel looked at Avery and turned away. His face was inches away from her face now. It seemed like she was uncomfortable. Rose couldn't tell if she was acting, or the unease was real.

Without warning, Avery put his right hand on Noel's waist and pulled her forward and kissed her.

Noel jerked back and let out a shriek.

Without warning, her right hand lifted in the air and came forward delivering a hard slap across his face. So loud it sounded like a lightning clap in the room.

Was that part of the script?

Erin bolted to her feet.

Apparently not based on that reaction.

Rose gasped.

Noel took several steps back.

Avery looked stunned.

"Are you crazy?" Erin shouted. "What did you do that for?"

Noel had her hand over her mouth. She looked at Erin, then at Rose, then at Avery. Back at Erin, who walked toward her with a purpose. Clearly angry.

"I'm so sorry," Noel said. "I didn't expect him to kiss me. I don't know why I slapped him. It all happened so fast."

Avery had a smirk on his face. His hand was on his cheek. When he moved it away, Rose saw a noticeable red mark.

Erin jerked the script out of Noel's hand.

"Get out of here! Now!" She pointed to the door.

Noel burst into tears and ran out of the room.

Rose stood there, frozen in place.

What in the world just happened?

6

"Am I getting fired?" I asked Rose, as we drove back to the office from the disastrous audition.

She was furious with me after I inexplicably slapped Avery Johnson across the face. Harder than I had intended. Actually, I didn't intend to slap him at all. It all happened so fast, I didn't have time to think through all the ramifications, which were becoming clearer now.

"I imagine we're both going to get fired," Rose said, with obvious pain behind the words.

"I'm sorry."

She didn't respond. Even when I ran into the bathroom sobbing right after it happened, she wasn't the least bit supportive. Didn't try to provide any comfort at all. Instead, told me to pull myself together. That the limo was leaving in five minutes with or without me.

"My acting career is over before it ever began," I said in the limo, refusing to burst into tears again. More water works wouldn't garner me any sympathy. It might even make her angrier.

For being so weak. I imagined her mother would be even less empathetic.

I feel like a fool.

"You've obviously burned the bridge with *Love Only*," Rose said. "Once you get a reputation as a problem in this industry, it's hard to recover from it."

"I'm not a problem."

"I'd say slapping the most popular actor on the planet would qualify as a problem."

"I didn't know he was going to kiss me."

"At first, I thought the kiss and slap were part of the script. When I saw Erin's reaction, I knew the slap wasn't supposed to happen."

"I wasn't thinking clearly. My instincts kicked in. I didn't even realize what I was doing."

She didn't say anything.

"I'm sorry," I said for the umpteenth time.

"Doesn't matter. What's done is done."

I had to bite my lip to hold back the tears. I was so embarrassed. My carousel of emotions went from embarrassment to anger at myself, to dread for what I knew was coming when we got back to the office.

How could I be so stupid?

By the time we walked into the lobby of the office building, the embarrassment had turned to shame. I'd let everyone down. Dr. McKinney, who referred me to Char. Char who took a chance on me. Rose, who took all that time to prepare me.

God.

That hurt the most. This morning I was on cloud nine. I had prayed and thanked him for opening this door for me. And I ruined it. Flushed my career down the toilet, in one lapse in judgment.

Avery Johnson kissed me. So what? He didn't mean anything by it. He was acting out the scene.

I didn't read anything about a kiss in the script.

If I'd been able to read the script ahead of time, I'd have been ready for it.

I'm going to get fired from the agency and black-balled in the industry. I'll be lucky to get a role in a local play somewhere.

Rose practically ran to her mother's office. That's how fast she walked after we got off the elevator. The door to the office was closed, but the assistant was at her desk.

"I need to see my mom, right away," Rose said, as coldly as a penguin in the Arctic.

"She's in a meeting."

Good. We can come back later.

Truthfully, I wanted to bolt out the door and never look back. Avoid the meeting altogether.

"Who's she meeting with?" Rose asked.

"Mrs. Williams and her daughter."

"Interrupt her. It's important."

The assistant immediately picked up the phone and dialed the number to Char's office.

"Sorry to disturb you," she said. "Your daughter needs to see you. She says it's urgent."

After a pause, she hung up the phone and said, "She'll be right out."

My heart sunk to the bottom of my chest. I don't think I'd ever dreaded anything this much in my entire life.

That's not true. Chris's funeral.

Nothing would ever be that bad. That's the hardest thing I'd ever done in my life.

I got through that. I can get through this.

The door opened about a minute later, and Char ushered a young girl and her mother into the reception area. The girl was cute. Looked to be about ten.

"I'll be in touch," Char said to the mother.

I hoped that meant she was done with the meeting, and we weren't disturbing her. Things were bad enough.

Rose pointed for me to enter the office first. Char's eyebrows raised, clearly wondering why her daughter treated me so aloofly.

I sat down in the chair next to the window, and Rose sat in the one next to me. What a difference a day made. This time yesterday, I sat in that same chair, a nervous but hopeful interviewee. Elated when Char agreed to take me on as a client. Before I could get my feet under me, I was back in the office, disgraced, like a schoolgirl in the principal's office, about to be kicked out for good.

Char took her place behind the desk. She leaned forward with her elbows firmly planted in the center of the desk.

"What happened?" she asked, in a tone that suggested it couldn't be that bad.

Oh yes it can.

Char looked at me, then Rose. Neither of us said anything.

Finally, Rose looked at me and said roughly, "Tell her!"

I licked my lips with my tongue. My mouth was suddenly parched like I'd been in the desert for three days.

"I slapped Avery Johnson," I said. The words seemed ridiculous even as I said them.

No noticeable facial reaction from Char.

"Okay," she said slowly. "Why did you do that, Noel?"

"Because he kissed me."

"I don't understand. Why would Avery Johnson kiss you?"

"I know!"

Rose suddenly felt the need to jump in and fill in the blanks. "Avery asked Noel to read lines with him. The scene called for him to kiss her. Which he did. She hauled off and slapped him across the face."

Char looked at me. "If he wanted to read lines with you, it's because he liked you. He rarely does that. It's because he was considering you for the part."

"I know that now."

"If he kissed you, it's because he wanted to see if you have chemistry as a couple."

"It caught me off guard. I wasn't expecting it."

Char flashed anger for the first time. Directed toward her daughter, not me. Which surprised me.

"I told you to prepare Noel for the audition!" she said.

"I did."

"Apparently not."

"So, this is my fault now!"

"Yes. You were responsible for making sure the audition went well."

"All Avery did was kiss her," Rose said, defensively.

"He didn't give me any warning," I said.

"Why did you have to slap him?" Rose said. "Just pull away if you're uncomfortable."

"It all happened so fast. I didn't know there'd be a kiss."

"Have you seen a *Love Only* movie?" Rose said to me rudely. "There's always a kiss."

"I've seen *Love Only* movies," I retorted, raising my intensity to match hers. Allowing my own anger surface. "I thought this was an audition to read lines. I didn't know I was going to have to make out with him."

"You're so naïve. You weren't making out. It was only a kiss."

The anger turned to tears which welled up to the surface before I could stop them. "Chris is the only person I've ever kissed in my entire life."

"That's ridiculous. You're a grown woman and you've only kissed one guy? I've kissed hundreds of guys and I'm not that much older than you."

Char gave Rose a look of disapproval.

"Well, not hundreds of guys," she backtracked. "I'm exaggerating. But I've kissed more than one guy."

"I'm telling the truth," I said. "Chris was the first guy I dated. I haven't even been on a date since he died. I told you that."

I flashed my hand to show them my rings, but then remembered that Rose told me to take them off for the audition. I reached in my pocket, pulled them out, and put them back on my finger.

"I haven't fully moved on from losing Chris," I said. "I'm not ready to be romantically involved with another man."

"You want to be an actress," Rose said. "You know you're going to have to kiss other guys. Everything about a *Love Only* movie leads to the final kiss."

"I knew if I got the part that I'd have to kiss Avery," I said between sobs that were mostly whimpers. "But I thought that was months from now. That I'd have time to prepare for it."

Char interjected, "I know for a fact that the academy has an entire week's curriculum teaching you how to act out love scenes."

I was embarrassed again.

"I know. I skipped that week."

"Why would you do that?"

"I wasn't ready. We had to pretend to make love to each other. The thought of it terrified me. So I told my teacher I had the flu."

"You're unbelievable," Rose said. A flash of disapproval crossed Char's face as she twisted her lips to the side and let out a groan.

"That's unfortunate. Most people are uncomfortable the first time. That's the reason for the class."

"I can fix this," I said. "I'll apologize to Mr. Johnson."

Char sat back in her chair. Staring at the ceiling. Thinking.

"No. I'll call Erin."

She punched a button on her phone, and her assistant answered through the intercom.

"Get Erin Palmer on the phone," Char said.

"I'll put her through when I get her," the voice from the other room answered.

The phone went silent. Char picked up a pen on her desk and began to tap it, staring out the window this time.

"She might not pick up," Rose said. "She's probably still in auditions."

My head lowered in shame. Things were getting worse by the minute. It's bad enough that I had to endure Char's and Rose's disapproval with me. Now, I'd have to endure Erin's wrath. I hoped she didn't pick up the phone. The last time I saw her, she ripped the script out of my hands and ordered me to leave. With eyes bulging out of her head. That's how mad she was. I doubted she had cooled down at all.

Why did I have to be there to listen to the conversation?

Just fire me and let me go on my way with my tail between my legs.

7

Everything was on hold as we waited to see if the assistant could get Erin on the line. If I could, I'd run out of the office and never look back.

I'd leave peacefully. Char could tear up the contract and I'd leave New York and go back to Philadelphia. At least I had a little bit of money from the lawsuit settlement. That's how I was able to afford to move to New York and take acting lessons. I wouldn't be destitute.

A few seconds later, the intercom exploded with sound and the assistant said, "I have Ms. Palmer on line four."

"Thank you."

Rather than pick up the handset, Char hit the speaker button. Probably for my benefit. So I could hear the two of them berate my behavior.

"Erin, we have a problem," Char said matter-of-factly.

"Yes, I'd say we do. I was just about to call you."

My heart skipped a beat when I heard Erin's voice.

"Good. I'm glad I'm not interrupting your auditions."

"I'm okay. We're on a lunch break. I guess you heard about the incident."

"I did. Why can't you control your client?" Char said. Which surprised me.

She's standing up for me?

Erin laughed. "My client? Your girl slapped Avery. She's the one who was out of control."

"After he tried to stick his tongue in her mouth."

I wanted to get Char's attention. He didn't stick his tongue in my mouth. I barely felt his lips on mine. I was so in shock.

I decided to keep quiet.

Erin laughed again. "I didn't see any tongue. They were acting out a scene in the movie. Avery was interested in your girl. So was I."

Was being the operative word.

"This isn't Avery's first rodeo," Char fired back. More sternly this time. "He should know better. One of the basic rules of an audition is that you don't touch the other person without their permission. Any first-year acting student knows that rule."

I remembered Dr. McKinney mentioning it in one of my classes.

"We did have your client's permission," Erin responded. "All the girls sign a disclaimer before they audition. It clearly states that we might ask them to read lines with another actor. A provision of the agreement gives said actor permission to kiss them. It doesn't happen often, but sometimes we want to see if there's chemistry between the couple."

Char looked at Rose, who shook her head.

"Noel never saw that document and certainly didn't sign it," Char stated.

"Hold on. Let me check her file."

The sound of papers rustled in the background.

"I guess you're right," Erin said, when she came back on the line. "I don't see it in the file. That's an oversight."

"That's not our oversight. My client didn't know she was going to be asked to kiss him, and Avery didn't ask permission before he did so."

"Did she have to assault him?" Erin said, clearly trying to make a joke.

Char laughed.

"Avery's ego can stand it. It wouldn't hurt for him to be taken down a notch."

"I don't disagree," Erin said. "I can't tell you how many times I've wanted to slap him. For different reasons. Nevertheless."

They both laughed.

She probably didn't know I was listening in on the conversation or she might not have been so openly disparaging about her actor. It told me Avery wasn't listening in to the conversation on the other end.

I wasn't laughing inside. While this wasn't how I figured the conversation would go, and I was thankful Char stood up for me, I still dreaded what she was going to say when she hung up the phone.

I had some hope though. The odds of me being fired had probably improved to about fifty-fifty. Better than when the conversation first started.

"Look Erin, we've known each other a long time. Noel feels bad about what happened."

I do.

"She agrees that she overreacted. Don't hold it against her. She's going to be a good actress someday."

I did overreact.

I wasn't sure about the good actress part. I still didn't believe that. Then I remembered that I got further than most people who didn't get asked to read lines with the most popular male actor on the planet. He was actually interested in me for the part.

"Give Avery a sincere apology from Noel and from me," Char added.

"That's the thing. Avery isn't mad. In fact, he's enthralled with Noel. He wants her for the part. He told me to call you and apologize for his behavior. To try and fix this."

My heart would have leapt across the room if it wasn't confined to my chest.

"Then let's do it."

"I don't know. I'm the one who is hesitating to offer her the role. I don't want any problems on the set."

"I give you my word that Noel won't be a problem. She's a delight to work with. As long as she knows what's expected of her and everyone treats her with respect and professionalism, we won't have any problems."

"All joking aside, Avery is the consummate professional. He's been with us for more than ten years. We've done more than twenty movies together. This is the first incident we've ever had like this."

"These are different times, Erin. With all the sexual harassment headlines, he might want to be more careful. Noel was never going to sue him, but she could've. He needs to ask first. Even if it's in the contract. Especially in an audition. The next girl might not be so understanding."

"Trust me. We will have that conversation."

"So, what do you think? Let's tie down a deal for Noel to star in your next movie."

Star!

I almost choked on my breath. I didn't think the word star would ever be used in the same sentence with my name.

Erin let out a huge sigh loud enough to fill the room.

"Twenty-five hundred dollars a week," she said.

"Five thousand. Twenty-week minimum."

"Meet me in the middle."

"Done."

"Three film option."

"Five thousand for second film. Ten thousand for third."

"That's a big jump for film three."

"It's your option. If you want her for a third film, it means you think she's worth it."

"Consider it done," Erin said. "Avery will be thrilled."

"Noel will be ecstatic."

I am!

Even though it still hadn't sunk in. Someone needed to pinch me. It's like I was having a dream. A nightmare with a happy ending.

"She really is good," Erin said. "You have something there."

"I know. That's why I sent her to you. I'll send you her contact information."

"We'll overnight her a script today. She'll have it tomorrow. It'll have the schedule in there as well."

"Excellent. Do you want to do dinner?"

"Yes! I'm suddenly free. Thanks to Noel, I don't have to sit through another eight hours of auditions. I can send all these girls home."

"I'll text you the time. We'll eat at the usual restaurant. My treat."

"Sounds good."

Char punched the button to disconnect the call with an extremely satisfied look on her face.

"Congratulations, Noel. Looks like you got yourself a role in a movie."

"I don't know what to say. Thank you. Thank you for everything. For sticking up for me. I can't tell you how much I appreciate it."

"This was a misunderstanding. You didn't do it on purpose."

"No, I didn't."

"Just don't do it again. One thing you'll learn about me, I have my client's backs. Within reason. Don't make me regret it."

"I won't let you down. I promise."

"By the way, there are worse things in life than kissing Avery Johnson."

I shuddered inside.

I guess I'm going to find out.

Sorry Chris.

8

The next day

The script arrived in the mail. I almost had a panic attack reading it. The movie was filled with intense romantic scenes. The role of Sarah required a deep emotional connection with Avery and a passionate kiss at the end.

Something I'd only experienced with Chris. I almost felt like I was cheating on him.

I had no idea how many times I'd have to kiss Avery in rehearsals and in filming, but I already dreaded it. I prayed about it. Asked God to give me peace.

God. Please help. I don't think I can do it. How do I kiss a total stranger? I'm not cut out to be an actress. I'm going to ruin everything.

Finally, I felt a still, small voice tell me to call Dr. McKinney, my professor at the acting academy. So, I did.

"I'm worried about the romantic scenes," I said to her. "Especially the kisses. My husband Chris is the only man I've ever kissed. I don't know how to have those kinds of feelings for a man who's not Chris."

"Noel, acting is not done in a vacuum. Every actor and actress draws upon their real-life experiences to get into the character."

"That's what I'm afraid of. I don't have any experiences like that. I didn't date a lot of guys. Actually, only one."

"Okay. But you do have experiences like that with Chris. You felt love for him hundreds of times. You can draw on that."

"How do I do that?"

"Pretend Avery is Chris."

That shocked me. It felt wrong. Like I was a fraud or something.

"It'll work," she said. "You're not the first person to be anxious about acting out a love scene. A lot of married people have to do a lot more than kiss on screen. It's a common practice to pretend it's your spouse that you're making love to."

I decided to try that strategy. When I practiced my lines, I pretended to talk to Chris. It seemed to work.

Would it work in real life?

It had to. I was under contract to complete the movie. Rehearsals would start soon. Filming right after that. I had no choice.

Avery was Chris.

* * *

May Rehearsals

Avery Johnson had fallen in love twenty-three times. Not coincidentally, the exact number of *Love Only* movies he'd starred in.

If you could call it love. One of his two sisters had quipped on more than one occasion that Avery wasn't a romantic but played one on the movie screen.

When rehearsals started for a new movie, he always fell head over heels in love with his co-star. As soon as the director said, "That's a wrap," the feelings dissipated into the wind like a puff of smoke from a pipe. By the final cast party, his co-star was just another woman to him. He had no romantic feelings for them at all.

That's how he knew the feelings weren't real. He wondered if the emotional roller coaster was why he hadn't found true love.

He was the youngest of seven kids. The last to get married. His mother said she would pray for him every day until he found a wife.

"I can't rush God's timing," Avery had said to her. "He'll bring me the right person at the right time."

"That's what I'm praying for. That God will bring the right person sooner rather than later and that you won't miss it when he puts her under your nose."

He wondered if his mother's prayers had finally been answered.

Noel Day captivated his emotions from the moment she stepped into that auditioning room in New York and opened her mouth to introduce herself. He had been looking down, bored, tired of the endless parade of bad actresses that they'd seen that day.

"My name is Noel Day," she had said, and his day was turned upside down. "I'm twenty-one. Five foot seven and a half inches tall."

His heart fluttered in his chest. He looked up and was mesmerized immediately. By her chocolate-brown hair that cascaded down to her shoulders in soft waves and glistened from the bright lights of the auditioning set.

Who was this person who sent an electric charge flowing through his body?

He almost blew it. He kissed her. She slapped him.

Erin went berserk and threw her out. Before Avery could stop her, Noel had run out of the room crying.

Avery wanted to go after her, but Erin advised against it.

"I want to apologize," he insisted.

"She should apologize to you," she said.

"It's not her fault. Call her and offer her the part. That'll fix it."

"I don't know. This girl might be a problem."

"I don't think so. She's perfect for the role. She's Sarah."

"I did like her."

When he got back from lunch, Erin said, "Her agent called, and the deal is done. Noel is Sarah. Rehearsals start in May."

They canceled the rest of the auditions, and Avery flew out of New York later that day. He had another movie to finish before May. Another woman to fall in love with. The whole time, he couldn't keep his mind off Noel.

When May finally arrived and he saw Noel for the first time in the rehearsal room, that same electricity was back. Something about that woman had captured his heart and hadn't let go even after all those months.

The room was filled with the entire cast mingling around a large table. He walked right up to Noel and held out his hand.

"It's good to see you again," he said warmly.

She flashed a friendly smile and said, "It's good to see you. Thank you for choosing me for the role. I'm so excited."

He could hear the excitement but also nervousness in her voice like she wanted to say something.

"Avery, I—"

"Noel, I need to apologize for my behavior at the audition," he said. "I'm sorry for kissing you without your permission."

She waved her hand in the air. "I'm the one who should apologize for slapping you."

"I deserved it. I'm glad you didn't have a sausage in your hand," he said, the line he had rehearsed for several weeks.

Her lips twisted to the side in confusion.

"That would've been the wurst," he said, making sure he had a broad smile on his face so she'd know he was kidding.

She didn't get the joke at first. In his head, he hadn't pictured it falling so flat.

"Bratwurst? Sausage? Get it? It's a joke."

She laughed dutifully.

"I'm glad you didn't hit me with a jigsaw," he added.

"Why?" she asked.

"Then I would've really been puzzled."

That time she genuinely laughed. Unless she was acting.

"How long have you been waiting to tell me those jokes?" she quipped.

"Why? Do you think I'm doing material now?"

"Sounds like it to me."

"Alright. I admit it. Those aren't my jokes. I found them on a bad joke's website."

"And that's where they belong."

"Ouch. That hurt. I was going to tell you a joke about boxing next, but it sounds like you don't want to hear the punchline."

"Ha ha. How long are you going to keep this up?" she asked.

"I've got a million of them."

"The next few days should be interesting," she said, with a cute smile.

"In all seriousness, I'm looking forward to working with you. You're a terrific actress."

Her cheeks flushed.

"Thank you," she said. "So are you." Her cheeks turned even redder. "Not an actress. I mean. You're a terrific actor."

They shared a deep laugh, and the tension left him as fast as a fastball leaving a pitcher's hand.

9

The week of rehearsals was usually the worst part of the process. Avery dreaded them. Ten-hour days. Sitting at a table, reading the lines until the director was satisfied.

Working with Noel made it one of the best weeks of his life.

Noel was even better than he thought she'd be. She was funny and quick-witted. Took instructions easily and incorporated suggestions effortlessly.

The director encouraged them to spend time together outside the set. To go on dates at night after rehearsals to build chemistry, but Avery never followed through. He always made up some kind of excuse.

He didn't trust himself. He had to hide his feelings from her. What if she rejected him? That'd ruin the whole movie.

Not only that, but Erin had warned him to be careful. Mentioned lawsuits. Sexual harassment.

He considered asking her to go to church with him. In his contract, he had a clause that said they wouldn't rehearse or film on Sunday mornings. He preferred to have the entire Sabbath off, but that wasn't possible. The cost of production was prohibitive. The production crew got paid whether they filmed or not. So he compromised with them.

Noel seemed to be a person of faith. She mentioned God and praying. Mostly in passing, but enough to where she seemed like a Christian.

Asking her to go to church with him didn't seem like the wrong thing to do, but he couldn't bring himself to ask.

What if she had a boyfriend? What if she didn't date coworkers? What if he took things too far and told her how he felt? If she rebuffed his advances, it'd make things awkward on the set and the director would notice.

Too many complications filled his head.

The consolation was that he could pour himself into the script which had many romantic scenes. He allowed himself to feel everything the character would feel. Let his love for her grow. His emotions were unleashed like water from a dam.

The best part was Noel wouldn't know the difference if she didn't feel the same way. His real feelings could be hidden behind the role. He could live vicariously through Kane. The character in love with Sarah.

Not Avery, in love with Noel.

The chemistry between them was intoxicating. He became confused. Noel matched his intensity. It seemed like she was falling for him as well, but he knew she might only be acting.

He asked around discreetly. As far as anyone knew, Noel wasn't dating anyone. Someone on the set had heard that she was married before but didn't know the details. That surprised Avery. Noel was only twenty-one. It seemed like she was too young to have been married and already divorced.

He was twenty-nine and wondered if the age difference would be a problem. Unfortunately, he wouldn't get the chance to find out because when rehearsals were over, everyone went their separate ways.

After a week apart from her, the feelings had only grown stronger. Avery was certain he was in love with her.

She seemed attracted to him as well, although he couldn't really tell since it's acting, by definition.

Could he tell her his real feelings? Not until the filming was over in June.

* * *

June
On The Set

Avery could hardly wait to see Noel again. The last few weeks of separation drove him crazy. Filming started, and it's like they hadn't skipped a beat. As each day passed, he found himself more and more hopelessly in love with her.

The director and Erin never noticed. Or if they did, they never said anything. They were pleased. Filming was completed in twelve days. Sometimes a scene only took one take. It all went by *too* fast, as far as he was concerned.

The last two scenes left to be filmed were the kissing scenes. The director saved those for the last day. He didn't want them kissing during rehearsal or on a date. He wanted their first kiss to be in front of the camera. In real time. As natural as possible. Neither of them told him they had kissed at the audition. If you could call it a kiss.

Avery had anticipated that day since the beginning of rehearsals. When it finally arrived, he was as nervous as a schoolboy with a crush. He barely slept the night before.

Shooting didn't start until midafternoon. The morning was torture as he had to endure the wait. He arrived at the set. When he saw Noel, he felt like someone had given him a dozen B12 shots.

He took up his position and she came and stood next to him. The director reminded them of a few things they'd already discussed at rehearsals and then took his seat next to the camera.

"Pretend you're in love. I want to see it in the camera," he said.

I won't have to pretend.

Of course, the set was filled with slews of people. Guests. Producers. Crew. Everyone who had anything to do with the movie attended the last day. The lights bore down on them. Several cameras pointed in their direction. Boom mics hovered overhead.

Not the least bit romantic. Everything was choreographed. The director moved their heads around, then walked behind the camera to look. Then repeated the process. That continued for nearly ten minutes. They had to stand with their lips inches apart for what seemed like an eternity while the director got the shot he wanted.

Not that Avery was complaining.

Thank God for breath mints.

The first kiss was from the same scene they had acted out at the audition under the mistletoe. He longed to get started. To feel her lips on his again. That's all he could think about.

"I promise I won't slap you this time," Noel whispered while they were frozen in place.

"That's good to hear," he said, moving his lips but trying not to move his head.

"Do you know how flowers kiss?" she asked, with a smile that sent chills down his spine.

"How?"

"With their tulips."

His head moved when he chuckled. "That's funny. Now who is the one doing material?"

"Don't move," the director said roughly.

They both became still as statues, although he could tell she tried to keep from laughing.

"We're good," the director finally said. "Are you ready?"

"Yes."

"And ... action."

Before he knew it, the kiss was over. The script called for it to be awkward and it was.

"We got it," the director said.

Avery felt a little disappointed. He wouldn't have minded acting out the scene a couple times. Maybe for the next one—the intense kiss that lasted more than a few seconds. The one he'd been looking forward to for days and dreading at the same time.

The last kiss was the money shot. Typical *Love Only* movie. Everything in the plot built up to that moment. The kiss had to be passionate and lasting. As the camera came close then faded away.

They changed to a different location on the other side of the street. Set up with fake snow. Avery had seen the budget. They spent around $50,000 to have the fake stuff brought in. Fortunately, they didn't have to do a wardrobe change.

The scene had no lines. Only the kiss. They stood in front of the courthouse in the town square. In each other's arms. Staring into each other's eyes.

The director said, "Action."

Avery suddenly felt extremely uncomfortable. His heart pounded so hard in his chest he could hear it in his ears.

He leaned in.

His lips quivered.

His touched hers.

Her lips were soft and warm. Inviting. She tasted minty.

He kissed her slowly at first. Then pulled her closer. Kissing her more deeply. Passionately. She responded with the same intensity. He'd crossed the line from acting to real life.

The director called out, "And ... stop!"

Their lips parted slowly. Almost lingering. He didn't want the kiss to end but stepped back. She looked up at him shyly. Her cheeks were flushed. She gently touched her lips, as if to ponder the moment.

The director said, "That's a wrap, everybody! Another one in the books."

The crew burst into applause. As did the bystanders, who cheered.

Avery took Noel's hand and turned to face everyone. They took a bow as the applause became more enthusiastic.

He turned and gave her a hug. "Thank you, Noel," he said. "You were terrific."

"You weren't so bad yourself," she said. "I loved every minute of it."

He wanted to unburden himself. Tell her how he felt. Now wasn't the time.

Before he knew it, she was gone. Whisked away by Rose to her trailer. They barely spoke at the afterparty. When he saw her, the feelings were still there. This had never happened to him before. That's how he knew his love for Noel was real.

What about her? He thought she kissed him like she was in love with him. He knew the difference. Or so he thought.

Was it real or was she acting?

10

Everything went well at the rehearsals and at the shoot. Even the kisses with Avery which I dreaded. The whole thing was a whirlwind and went so fast it felt like a blur to me.

Erin Palmer came up to me at the afterparty to thank me.

"You were terrific, Noel," she said. "And we finished ahead of schedule. That'll make a lot of people happy. Good job."

"Thank you for giving me the chance. I hope you ask me to do another movie for you."

"We definitely will. I already have something in mind."

"With Avery?"

Noel looked across the room and saw him. He was surrounded by a group of people. The afterparty was almost over and they hadn't said more than a couple words to each other.

I guessed that's how the movie business worked. It felt weird being so close to him for so many weeks and now they were nothing more than acquaintances. Someone she knew from work.

"Avery's booked up through the next year with other movies," Erin said. "I have another script I want you to read. It's set in Aspen, Colorado. We'll shoot this fall. I'll talk to Char."

"That's great. I look forward to it."

"That last kiss between you and Avery was off-the-charts good. The movie is going to be a hit. The public is going to love you with him."

"Avery was a pleasure to work with. And a perfect gentleman."

"You looked so natural together."

Dr. McKinney's strategy had worked to perfection. When we got to the kisses, I closed my eyes, pictured Chris, and gave myself to it.

After the last kiss, I was confused. It felt like a real kiss. Like Avery really *was* in love with me. It felt like it did when Chris kissed me.

A month later, I noticed that I was still thinking about Avery. I wondered if I had fallen in love with him.

Was it Avery I loved or Kane, the character he played?

Or Chris? The confluence of Avery and Chris I had concocted in my mind had blurred my senses.

What about Avery? How did he feel about me?

Was it real or was he acting?

12

Five months later

"I have good news," Char said to me on the phone.

"I love good news," I said.

I was in Aspen, Colorado. We'd wrapped up shooting my second movie with *Love Only*. In a few minutes, I'd get dressed for the afterparty. Tomorrow morning, I planned to catch a flight back to New York. Satisfied that I'd successfully finished another project for them.

Hopefully, they'd pick up the option for the third movie. That's what I was praying for. Believing God for. I had no reason to think they wouldn't.

Perhaps the good news was related to a third movie.

"*Love Only* has chosen yours and Avery's movie as the showcase for the Christmas holidays," Char said.

"What does that mean?"

"*Love Only* picks one movie per Christmas and puts all their publicity behind it. To advertise their Christmas line up. It means your face is going to be plastered all over the country. On billboards. Magazine covers. This is big for your career."

"That's amazing."

"Erin Palmer sent me the press release. The *Very Merry Countdown to Christmas* starts November first and features forty-four *Love Only* movies.

Nine originals including yours. Out of those forty-four, they must think yours is the best. Or at least the most marketable."

"I can't believe it."

"You and Avery are going to do a promotional tour together."

Up until that point, I was excited but also tired from all the long hours of shooting. When she mentioned Avery's name, my heart raced and my blood pumped harder, sending a hot rush to my head.

Strange since I'd barely thought about Avery for three months.

Before I could ask for more specifics, she said, "There's more. You'll like this news even better."

"How's that possible?"

"They want you for a third film."

"Yeah!"

"You'll be starring with Avery again."

My already racing heart did gymnastics in my chest. I'd been sitting down on the couch. I bolted up and paced around the room.

"A third movie? This one with Avery? Tell me more."

The thought of doing another movie with Avery sent a wave of desire through my body. Did I still have feelings for him? After the last movie, I thought I might. Then I poured myself into the second movie and a new leading man and the feelings went away.

Now they were back in bushels.

What did that mean?

I didn't have time to analyze it, but I did know that I couldn't let Char see me overexcited. She'd start asking questions I wasn't prepared to answer.

"Rehearsals start in January," Char said. "Another Christmas movie. This time for a Christmas in July release."

Then I remembered. "Erin said that Avery was booked through next year with movies and that I wouldn't be doing one with him that soon."

"He was. The girl they cast for the movie is out. You're in."

"Aww. I feel bad for her."

"Oh, my dear Noel. You're so naïve. You've got to learn to be more cutthroat."

"I can feel happy for myself and sad for her at the same time."

"Whatever. I don't represent her, so I don't feel bad for her at all."

"I am excited to be working with Avery again."

Based on the exhilaration pumping through my body, I was more than excited. I was downright giddy.

"How can I ever thank you?"

"Keep putting out good movies. Speaking of which, are you finished filming in Colorado?"

"Yes. I'm looking out my hotel room window at Aspen mountain. The movie is finished. The afterparty is tonight."

"How'd it go?"

"Great."

"Rose said it was going well."

My second film was called *Head Over Skis*. I was a ski instructor at Aspen Lodge. A wealthy businessman hired me to give him private lessons. Of course, sparks flew, and a romance blossomed. The movie ended with a kiss.

Thankfully, I only had to kiss him once.

I wasn't as attracted to him as I was to Avery.

Where did that thought come from?

He wasn't as good an actor as Avery either and we took several takes to get the kiss right. So technically, I kissed him more than once. Luckily, I had my strategy. Pretend he was Chris.

He wasn't as good a kisser as Avery though.

Oh, my word!

I had Avery on my brain now. I thought I was finally over him. Apparently not.

While my thoughts wandered to Avery, Char was still talking. Giving me instructions. I hoped I remembered them all.

"Take a couple weeks off," Char said. "Go lay on a beach somewhere and work on your tan. Then come back refreshed and ready to go back to work. I need you in L.A. on December first for the premiere."

"L.A.?"

I'd never been to Los Angeles before.

"They're doing a premier screening in Hollywood. At Grauman's Chinese Theatre. Red carpet and everything. You'll meet Avery there."

"December first. Got it."

Avery's going to be there!

"Actually, December first is the screening. You need to get there the day before. Rose will meet you."

"My first red carpet. I'm so excited."

"Your first of many, I would guess."

I hung up the phone slowly. Not sure what I was most shocked by. A premiere. The showcase.

Another movie with Avery!

I still hadn't sat down. I paced around my hotel suite like a tiger in a cage waiting for a meal.

Did Avery request me for the movie?

The last time I spoke to him was at the afterparty in June. About a week after I got back to New York, a bouquet of flowers showed up on my door with a cute note. Three dozen tulips. They made me laugh. As did the card.

I hope you enjoy your tulips as much as I enjoyed your two lips. Ha! Love Avery.

Until next time.

He drew a heart above his name.

The note seemed a little odd at first. He used the word *love*. Then I decided it meant nothing to him. He probably sent all his co-stars flowers after the movie was finished.

His assistant probably wrote the note.

Even if his assistant wrote it, Avery had the idea for tulips. No one else knew about the private joke but him.

Still, I tried not to read too much into it. The gesture was nice. That's all it was. When a few months passed and I hadn't heard from him, I tried not to be disappointed and poured myself into the second movie.

The phone was still in my hand. I looked up Grauman's Chinese Theatre and was shocked to learn that they hosted some of the biggest movie premieres in the world. All the major motion picture companies released their blockbuster hits there.

There'd be press. Paparazzi. Limousines. A red carpet.

And Avery.

Why am I so nervous to see him?

13

Los Angeles

For the first time in my brief acting career, I felt like a movie star. I got off the plane and Rose was outside security to meet me along with half a dozen paparazzi who furiously snapped my picture while I awkwardly posed.

To my further surprise, a crowd formed to see what all the hoopla was about and asked for my autograph. After a few minutes of a steady stream of new people, Rose whisked me away to an awaiting limousine while she had someone get my bags.

"None of those people who asked for my autograph even know who I am," I said, after we settled in the limo and sped away.

"After tomorrow they'll know."

She proceeded to tell me the schedule.

"This afternoon, you have a fitting for your dress. A major designer made it for you. This evening you'll meet with the publicist for the event. You'll learn the ins and outs of what's expected of you tomorrow."

"When will I see Avery?"

The question erupted out of my mouth like a burp before I even had a chance to tone down the excitement behind it.

"He'll meet us in the lobby tomorrow afternoon. You'll ride in a limo with him to the premiere, and the two of you will basically be joined at the hip the rest of the afternoon. You'll have a backstage meet and greet with some dignitaries. You'll pose for pictures, sign autographs, schmooze the people who paid a lot of money to meet you and Avery."

I laughed. "They want to meet Avery. I doubt anyone would pay money to see me."

"You'd be surprised. Avery has his following, but a lot of people are anxiously waiting to see who the next *Love Only* starlet is."

"I'm hardly a starlet. I do hope they like the movie and they like me. That's the main thing."

"They will. I'm told the movie is fabulous. It has to be, or they wouldn't have chosen it for the premiere."

"I suppose. It seemed good while we were filming it."

"After the meet and greet, you and Avery will sit through the screening with about eight or nine hundred people. I'm told it's sold out. Oh, I forgot. There's the red carpet. When you arrive, you and Avery will pose for pictures. Do television interviews. Then go to the meet and greet."

"I don't really know how to act on the red carpet."

"That's why you're meeting with the publicist tonight. To go through everything. If you have any questions, bring them up then."

"I will."

"After the movie screening, you'll have more hobnobbing with your adoring fans in the lobby of the theatre. More pictures, etc. Then you'll come back to the hotel. On Sunday, you and Avery will tape several talk shows and talk about the Christmas movie and the new movie that'll be out in July. On Monday, you'll fly back to New York with Avery to tape the talk shows there and make a number of promotional appearances around the city."

I'm going to fly to New York with Avery? We'd never spent a single minute alone.

This should be interesting.

* * *

The next afternoon

I didn't realize how much I looked forward to seeing Avery until the time came. His face lit up when he saw me. Was he playing for the cameras or was he happy to see me as well?

I smiled broadly to match his expression. My tight-fitting dress that went to the floor prevented me from rushing to his side. When I got there, he kissed me on the cheek.

"Hello, Noel," he said warmly. "It's so good to see you again. I've missed you."

I didn't know how to take that last statement.

"Thank you," was all I could get to come out of my mouth.

The lobby of the hotel was abuzz with people standing behind a roped line on both sides of the lobby. The paparazzi roamed free and snapped pictures of us from all angles. Avery took my arm so that we faced them.

I decided to take my cues from him. He led us over to the crowd behind the ropes, and we shook hands and posed for pictures with the fans, who I was certain had no idea who I was other than that I was the lady on the promotional posters. I hadn't seen them, but Rose said my picture was on a dozen billboards around Los Angeles.

After a few minutes of mingling with the crowd, the publicist said we had to go. Avery took my arm as we walked outside to the awaiting limo where more fans had gathered. His hand moved to the small of my back, directing my steps to the opened door, and sending a chill down my spine.

Once we were alone in the car, I thought I'd be able to catch my breath, but I found myself even more nervous. The tight-fitting dress contributed to my restricted breathing. That and being alone with Avery for the first time terrified me.

"How have you been?" he asked, flashing his dimples.

"I've been well. I just finished a movie in Aspen, Colorado."

"Who was that with?"

I heard a hint of jealousy behind the question, but I dismissed the thought. I had to be reading more into it than was actually there.

"Miles Bennett," I said.

He nodded several times like a bobblehead doll. I wasn't sure if he approved or not.

"I'm looking forward to January and working with you again," he said, clearly wanting to change the subject.

"Me too."

An awkward silence ensued. I was told the drive was about twenty minutes.

"How 'bout this premiere?" I said. "They chose our movie. Isn't it wonderful?"

"I figured they would."

"Why's that?"

"They've chosen one of my movies for four straight years, and I did three movies this year. This was the only Christmas movie."

"Hmm."

"Would you like to have dinner with me afterward?" he blurted. "I have something I want to talk to you about."

It caught me totally off guard. Too much to process at once.

Did I have any responsibilities? I tried to remember.

Did I want to dine alone with him? This was awkward enough.

What did he want to talk to me about?

My mind spun like the waiting cursor on a computer. The spinning beach ball of death as they called it. That's sort of how I felt in the moment. So much so that I didn't answer right away.

"That's if you don't already have plans," he added.

"I'd love to have dinner with you. If Rose doesn't have something for me to do. I can't think of anything off the top of my head."

"That's great. I know a terrific restaurant. We'll have a private table. It'll give us a chance to be alone."

"Sounds great."

"It's settled then."

Why does he want to be alone with me?

14

Avery had lobbied for his movie with Noel to be the showcase. He wanted her to be at the premiere because he decided to tell her he was in love with her. Now that they were there, the problem was figuring out how to get her alone. That's when he came up with the idea of dinner after the screening.

Telling her was risky. He wasn't sure what to expect. His advances might be totally rebuffed. That's a chance he had to take. It had to be done before the next movie. He'd be hurt if she didn't feel the same way, but at least he'd know, and he'd have a few weeks to get over her before they started rehearsals.

When she saw him for the first time at the hotel, her face lit up. She was obviously excited. Was that because of the premiere or because she was excited to see him?

He'd soon find out, one way or the other.

The premiere went well. The movie was great, and the fans loved it. They received a standing ovation at the end. The fans adored Noel. She handled herself like a star and stunned them in her chiffon-colored designer dress.

Once they got to their private table at the restaurant, she didn't seem as nervous. He was the one who was nervous now.

He wanted to get it over with, but this wasn't the kind of thing that could be rushed. He'd try and feel her out first. See if he could pull it out of her by asking questions. If she said she had a boyfriend, for instance, then he'd save himself the embarrassment of pouring out his feelings to unrequited love.

After some small talk that lasted through the salad course, he finally said the question that had been on his mind for months, "How come a pretty girl like you hasn't been snatched up by someone already?"

"How come a handsome guy like you hasn't been snatched up by someone already?"

Clever. Turning the question on him.

"I haven't found the right person yet," he answered.

"It shouldn't be hard. You must have women throwing themselves at you."

"I did three movies this year. I barely had time to turn around twice. Much less go to the trouble of finding a date, taking her out, then wooing her. I'm not the kind of guy that goes for a one-night stand or has a woman in every city, so things are pretty dry for me on the dating front. This is my first date in a while."

Her eyes widened. He immediately regretted calling this a date.

"Interesting. I can see how that'd be hard."

"How about you? Do you date much back in New York?" he asked.

"Not really."

She took a nervous drink from her glass. This was going to be harder than he thought.

"Actually, I haven't been on a date in nearly three years," she said.

He could hardly contain his excitement.

"My last date was with my husband," she said. Her eyes squinted and she crinkled her nose. She stared at him as if she were looking for a reaction.

"Really," he said, pretending not to know that information. He'd heard through the grapevine that her husband had died on their honeymoon. He didn't know the details.

"His name was Chris. He died on our honeymoon three years ago this month."

"I'm so sorry to hear that." His heart hurt for her when he heard the pain behind the words.

"What was Chris like?" he asked.

"A lot like you. A really nice guy. He had blue eyes and dimples like you."

"He must've been a great guy to have captured your heart."

"That's why it's been hard for me to start dating again. Some people tell me I should. Like you, finding the time is harder now that I'm doing movies."

"People say we'd make a good couple," he said. "That we look good together in pictures, I mean."

He was mentally kicking himself for having so little confidence to say what he really felt.

She nodded.

"We have a chemistry on the set, don't you think? I really like you. Um. Working with you."

She got a sheepish grin on her face. "You want to hear a secret," she said, as she leaned toward him. "I haven't told anyone this."

His heart beat even faster. Like he'd been on a rowing machine for an hour.

Was she going to tell him that she had feelings for him? That'd make things so much easier if she did.

"At first, I was worried about our romantic scenes."

He leaned forward in his chair.

"My acting teacher told me to pretend that you were Chris. To picture him when we kissed."

An uncontrollable wave of hurt came over him like a tsunami. It felt like he'd been stabbed in the heart.

She didn't have feelings for him at all.

The whole thing had been a ruse. All that time, he thought she was falling in love with him, but she wasn't. The kisses were passionate and seemed real, but they weren't.

She was thinking about her dead husband. That's who she was kissing. Not him.

He was suddenly furious. He bit his lip to keep from letting his true feelings be known.

Exploding in anger would be extremely inappropriate. Especially in the restaurant. He didn't want to cause a scene. The paparazzi were right outside the door.

He had to get out of there before he said something he deeply regretted.

He needed an excuse.

He pulled out his phone and pretended he got a text.

"I'm sorry, Noel," he said. "I'm going to have to cut this evening short. Something has come up."

"We haven't even gotten our food."

"Don't worry about it. I'll cover the bill. I have to go."

Her mouth flew open in disbelief. "I can go with you."

"No. I'm sorry. You stay. I have to go. You can take the limo back."

He stood and walked away before she could answer. Without looking back.

He walked briskly through the restaurant and out the door to a barrage of paparazzi flashing pictures. He hailed a cab and got away as quickly as he could.

Totally devastated.

Feeling completely rejected.

It would've been better had she flat out said she wasn't interested in him. To pretend she had feelings for him while she was only thinking about another man was the most hurtful thing he'd ever experienced in his life.

The whole trip back to the hotel, he was torn. Part of him was angry at Noel. The other part hurt. Mostly feeling like his hopes were dashed. This was the first person he'd ever really been interested in.

His mom's prayers would continue to go unanswered. Good thing he hadn't mentioned Noel to her. He almost did.

When he walked in the lobby of the hotel, Erin sat in a chair. She bolted up as soon as she saw him. The paparazzi entered behind him so he walked past her not stopping headed straight for the elevator. She followed him in.

"I didn't expect to see you so soon," she said. "Is your date over already?"

"It wasn't a date. We just had dinner."

"Where's Noel?"

"She's still at the restaurant."

"You left her there alone? Why?"

"I don't want to talk about it."

"What's wrong?"

"I don't think I can do the next movie with her."

He immediately regretted saying the words.

"Why? Did the two of you have some kind of fight? Did she slap you again?"

He grimaced. It felt like she had ripped his heart out of his chest.

"I was only kidding," Erin said.

They reached the top floor. He stepped off the elevator and practically ran to his room. Erin somehow matched his steps.

"Can we talk about it?" she said, with growing intensity.

"No. I'll finish the promotional tour with Noel. Then I'm done. But don't say anything to her right now. Let's tell her later. After the tour. Let her down easy."

"I don't understand—"

"Good night."

Avery closed the door behind him.

15

I'd barely been back from the restaurant when a knock on my hotel door startled me.

Avery?

I opened the door and Rose bolted into the room. Like her pants were on fire.

"What happened at the restaurant?" she asked in a demanding voice.

"What do you mean?"

"Mom called a minute ago and said she got a text from Erin. She said something happened between you and Avery at the restaurant but didn't say what. Mom told me to come to your room and find out what it was."

Panic shot through my entire body. Avery must've said something to Erin. *But what?*

My mind was a whirlwind of thoughts. Rather than speculate, I told her what I knew.

"I don't know what happened," I said. "Avery got a text and had to leave. He didn't say why. It didn't have anything to do with me."

Since I was hungry, I thought about staying but left right after him. I was relieved when the limo was still parked in front. Also that the paparazzi were gone. On the drive back to the hotel, I wracked my brain trying to make sense of what had happened. The conversation replayed in my head a dozen times.

Did I say something to offend him?

I eventually decided that Avery had an emergency and that's why he left in such a hurry. I certainly didn't do or say anything wrong.

If anything, Avery was the one acting weird. Asking me about my dating life. Like he was fishing for information.

When I brought up Chris, that's when he got up and left. Was that somehow related? Why would me talking about Chris upset him?

Rose paced the room which made me more nervous.

"My mom is going to kill me if I screwed this up."

"You didn't do anything. Why would your mom be mad at you?"

"She won't see it that way."

Rose's phone rang interrupting our conversation.

"Hi Mom. I'm here with Noel. I'll put you on speaker."

"What did you do?" Char said accusingly.

My heart skipped two beats. Was she talking to me?

"I didn't do anything," I answered without any conviction behind the words.

"What did you say to Avery?" Char asked roughly.

"I don't know what you're talking about."

"I got a call from Erin Palmer. She was practically hysterical. She said that Avery wants to replace you in the movie."

"What? Replace me! Why would Avery want to replace me?"

My mind reeled out of control. None of this made sense.

"That's what I'm trying to find out."

I tried hard not to get defensive. It might make it look like I did something wrong.

"Avery asked me to dinner. It was his idea. We were having a pleasant conversation when he got a text. He apologized and said he had to leave. I guess he caught a cab because he left the limo for me. I just got back to my hotel room. I'm as bewildered as you are."

"Apparently you did something if he wants to replace you in the movie."

"Can he do that?"

"Of course, he can. He did that to the first girl. He can do that to you."

"Did he say why he doesn't want to work with me anymore?" Tears built up in my eyes. From anger and also from the hurt.

"He wouldn't say. All she knew was that he was upset. She'd never seen him like this."

I was crying now.

"Why would he replace me? That's not fair. I was perfectly nice to him."

"And where were you, Rose?" Char exploded. "You were supposed to be watching Noel. To keep something like this from happening."

"What am I supposed to do? Go on a date with them. I'm not a chaperone."

"It wasn't a date," I said, choking back the tears. I remembered how I felt when Avery said it was a date. My cheeks had flushed and part of me loved hearing he thought it was a date.

"I'll deal with you later, Rose. Right now, I'm in damage control mode. It doesn't sound like this can be fixed."

"What do you want us to do?" Rose said.

"Hang tight. Hopefully, Erin can talk some sense into Avery first thing in the morning. Maybe she can find out what has him so upset."

"I'll do whatever they want me to do," I said. "They have to know it's not my fault."

"It won't matter what you say. Trust me, if they must choose between you and Avery, they'll choose Avery a hundred out of a hundred times. He's their gravy train and the network's biggest star. You are replaceable."

"I'm sorry," I said, even though I didn't know what I was sorry about.

"I told you I'd have your back within reason," Char said. "Since I don't know what you did, I don't know if you did anything wrong. Maybe tomorrow, cooler heads will prevail, and we can get this train back on the tracks."

"I hope so," I said, but Char had already hung up.

Rose still paced.

"This is a disaster," she said. "My mom hates me."

"She's your mother. She doesn't hate you."

"She does. She doesn't think I can do the job. Just when things were going so well. I've been working for her all these years, and I still haven't brought her a star. I thought you had that potential. I guess that was too good to be true."

"It's not your fault. I don't know whose fault it is, but it's definitely not yours."

"My mom won't see it that way."

"I'll talk to her."

"You need to get some sleep. Hopefully, this whole thing blows over tomorrow."

Before I could say anything further, Rose headed for the door. As quickly as she had come, she was gone, leaving me to sort out the eddy of emotions that thrashed around inside of me.

I felt like I was alone in the ocean drowning under a sea of emotions and no one was going to throw me a lifeline.

Had I ruined my career? *Again!*

I started to pace the same path Rose had taken. The more I did, the angrier I got. I had a few choice words for Avery who I blamed for the drama.

"Of all the nerve! Who do you think you are? Taking me off your movie. You might be a big star, but you can't play with people's emotions and their careers like that!"

I made a path to the bedroom of my suite then back to the kitchen, through the living room and dining room and back to the bedroom. Then repeated the path. Keeping up my diatribe with him.

"You were the one acting weird, Mister!"

I began to speak in a mocking voice. Imitating his words.

"Why is a pretty girl like you still single?"

"Do you date much in New York?"

"None of your business who I date."

I regretted answering his questions at the restaurant. Who I date is my own business. I barely know the man.

Calm down, Noel.

"I won't calm down. He owes me an explanation."

"I'm going to his room right now and demand to know why he took me off the movie."

16

Avery's room was on the same floor as mine. The top floor of the hotel had four suites. A presidential suite, which was Avery's room, a governor's suite, and then two junior suites. I had one of the juniors.

I stomped out of my room and pounded on his door, even though it was after ten at night.

"Avery! It's Noel. We need to talk."

He didn't answer.

"I know you're in there."

Actually, I didn't, but it sounded tough and like something I'd seen in the movies.

Silence.

I knocked harder when he didn't answer.

"Avery, open the door. I know why you're mad at me. Let's talk about it."

Still nothing.

What if he has a girl in the room?

I laughed. *Unlikely.*

What if he calls the cops?

I chuckled again and answered my own questions. Avery said he wasn't the kind to go for a one-night stand. Calling security might be a possibility. If I was wrong about my theory, then I might spend the night in jail. My behavior was borderline stalking.

What would Char think about having to bail me out of jail? The paparazzi would be all over it.

Scandalous.

"Erin said you don't want me on the movie. Don't you think you owe me an explanation?"

I heard a noise come from inside the room. A lock clicked. The door opened.

When Avery didn't appear in the doorway, I stepped inside into a large, opulent room. It had a large dining table on the left with a bar and kitchen area and a huge living room and fireplace on the right. The room was dimly lit by one lamp in the living room. Avery stood a few feet from the door, wearing shorts and a tee shirt. No shoes. Looking pretty buff, momentarily distracting me.

I stepped completely in and closed the door behind me.

"Can we talk?" I asked, softening my tone.

He walked away from me toward the living room.

"Why did you ask me at the restaurant if I was dating someone?"

"I was making small talk."

"Why did you get so upset when I mentioned Chris?"

He still had his back to me but had stopped walking. It seemed like he didn't want me to see his expression.

I put my hand on his back when he stopped.

"You did it because you have feelings for me, don't you?" I said, gently.

He didn't answer.

I took his arm and turned him around, so he faced me. Tears had welled up in his eyes which confirmed what I already knew. It warmed my heart and I felt bad for him at the same time as I understood why he had behaved so strangely.

"Are you in love with me?" I said, sweetly.

He turned away again.

I took his hand and led him to the couch and sat down with him.

"Why didn't you tell me?" I said, keeping my hand on his.

He chuckled nervously. "I wanted to. A million times. I was afraid you didn't feel the same way. I star in romance movies, and I can't even talk to a woman in real life. It's easier for me to say movie lines, than real ones."

"Can I explain what I meant by what I said?"

"You don't owe me an explanation. You don't feel the same way about me. It's not you, it's me."

"That does sound like a line from a movie."

His face was deeply pained. His head slumped down. His lips curled into a frown. His eyebrows narrowed, and his eyelashes were wet from the tears. Every muscle on his face seemed to be tense.

I had really hurt him. I could see why now.

"I thought Chris was the love of my life. That he was my soulmate. That God brought us together. When he died … I didn't think I'd ever love anyone again."

My tears tried to escape my eyes now. At some point, I might not be able to hold them back.

"I can't compete with the memory of your husband." His voice cracked as he said it.

"It's not a competition, Avery. I'm sorry I told you what my acting teacher told me to do. That was insensitive. I shouldn't have said it. I don't know what I was thinking."

"You were thinking that you didn't know how to kiss a stranger and asked her for advice. I get it."

"Right. But it's more than that. I wasn't sure how to manufacture feelings for you. To pretend that I was in love with you."

He grimaced. I could tell my words still hurt him.

"I know it's acting, but the romantic scenes scared me."

He nodded like he understood.

"I'm messed up. I've been having a hard time getting over my grief. When you kissed me at the audition, I panicked. That's why I slapped you. I was afraid of getting that close to someone. It's like I was doing something wrong."

"I apologized for that. I shouldn't have kissed you."

"I know. And I accepted your apology. But when I got the part in the movie, I didn't know if I would be any good at acting like I was in love with a total stranger. So, like you said, I called my acting coach for advice."

"It was hard for me at first too. It's still hard. I don't think you ever really get used to it. I don't know how married couples do it."

"Exactly. That's what I'm trying to make you understand. I still feel like I'm married. I wear my wedding rings. The only reason I didn't wear them to the audition was because Rose told me to take them off. Of course, I couldn't wear them on the set or on the promotional tour."

"I didn't know."

"It's easier for me to pretend I'm still married than to let myself have feelings for someone else. That's what made it hard for me to get close to you."

"I didn't expect to fall in love with you."

"I didn't know you were in love with me."

"At first, I didn't know either. Then I realized the feelings were real. I'd never felt that way before. I should've said something, but I figured they'd go away. They never did. When I saw you earlier today in the lobby, I realized that I was still in love with you. That's why I wanted to talk to you alone. To tell you."

"And I said what I said about Chris and ruined everything."

"It's not your fault. I don't expect you not to love Chris. I get why you do. A part of you will always love him."

"Yes, I will."

"Will there ever be room in your heart for someone else?"

"I think there is."

His eyes brightened. "Do you think someday it might be me?"

I smiled. He sounded like a shy schoolboy.

"That's what I wanted to tell you at the restaurant. You didn't let me finish my thoughts. Even though I was thinking about Chris when I kissed you—"

He grimaced again and the smile was gone.

I put my finger on his lips.

"What I was going to say is ... even though I was thinking about Chris when we kissed, I realized over time that my feelings are for you, not Chris."

His tears dried up momentarily.

"You have feelings for me?"

"I do."

"Since when?"

"They started while we were filming. I found myself falling in love with you, but I was confused."

"I didn't know you were in love with me. I thought you were acting."

"I thought *you* were acting."

Before I knew it, his lips were pressed against mine. I pulled back.

"I'm sorry," he said. "I did it again. I shouldn't have kissed you."

I put his cheeks between both of my hands, and I kissed him. Hard. Unleashing the passion that had been bottled up inside of me for three years.

He wrapped his arms around me, and I moved my arms, so they were around his neck. The kisses became softer. Just as intense, but more loving. Like we were trying to bring healing to each other. In a way we were.

I was out of breath by the time we stopped.

17

The next morning

Avery and I didn't kiss again that night. Instead, we sat on the couch and talked. About everything. God. Children. Our future. Our hopes and dreams. It's like we tried to fit months of dating into a few hours.

"I think we have it backwards," Avery joked. "Normally, couples date for months, then they say I love you. Technically, we've never even been on a date."

"We dated in the movie."

"And we can date in our next movie."

"Does this mean you want me to be in your movie after all?"

"Yes. I'm not very happy with Erin right now. She wasn't supposed to say anything. You weren't supposed to know. Not right away. I can't stand that I hurt you in that way. I'm sorry."

"You're forgiven. I'm sorry I said what I said about Chris. It was cruel."

"I forgive you too. I know you didn't mean it the way I took it."

Late in the evening, I fell asleep. When I woke, I had a blanket over me. Avery was gone. I couldn't find him anywhere in his suite.

I slipped out to the hallway and into my room.

Before I had a chance to do anything other than brush my teeth and lament how my hair looked in the mirror, I heard a knock on my door.

Rose walked in with a smile on her face.

"Hello, Rose," I said.

She looked me up and down. I still wore the designer dress I had on the night before.

"I fell asleep on the couch," I said. The truth. I didn't say whose couch I fell asleep on.

She nodded without any questions and walked across the room with a bounce in her step.

"My mom called. She said Erin called her this morning. I guess everything is resolved. The movie is back on. You need to get dressed. We're meeting Avery in the lobby in an hour."

"That's great!" I tried to act like I didn't already know.

"I don't know what happened, but all is forgiven. You're back in Avery's good graces."

We kissed and made up, I wanted to say but bit my tongue.

As to how far into his good graces, you don't know the half of it.

We're in love.

* * *

Rehearsals for *A Christmas to Remember* were scheduled to start in three weeks. After the promotional tour was finished, Avery and I barely had time to fit in what we wanted to get done between now and then.

Mainly, we wanted to spend as much time together as possible and get to know each other. It dawned on me that I didn't really know him. He lived in Nashville and his family in Michigan, so I combined the trips. Flew to Nashville first to see where he lived and go with him to his church.

When I got to Nashville, I was shocked. A casual observer wouldn't know Avery was a multi-millionaire several times over. His house was in a gated community, but modest. He lived in the secure neighborhood only because of his fame. He owned a reasonably priced five-year-old model SUV that only had seventeen thousand miles on it. Without any of the added extras he could've gotten.

"I'm never at home," he said, when I questioned him about it. "The car sits in the garage most of the time. Why would I need a fancy car and a mansion? It's just me. All I want is a place to sleep and shower and a dependable car. I can't see spending a lot of money when what I have will do."

I loved that humility in him. Even though I shouldn't have been surprised. He didn't wear fancy jewelry or clothes on the set. He certainly didn't act like a famous movie star. The film studio provided interns to wait on us and be at our beck and call. I remembered Avery poured his own coffee once and Erin chastised him.

"It's their job," she said.

"The coffee is right here," he argued. "I'm ten steps away from it. I'm perfectly capable of pouring my own coffee. I don't even need an intern. It's a waste of money."

"Interns are volunteers," Erin retorted. "They work for free so they can learn the ins and outs of the trade. Put them to work. If not for you, then for their benefit."

I'd overheard the conversation and been amused at the time. As I got to see the deeper side of Avery's personality, I saw where his lack of guile came from. He was a deeply religious man. His father was a pastor, and he grew up in church.

Much to my delight. That's something I worried about when we kissed and he told me he loved me in his room that night. I couldn't be unequally yoked with him. Turned out he was as strong in his faith as I was, if not stronger.

When we went to his church, Avery was treated like everyone else. He said he insisted the pastor and staff not give him any special treatment. It's like the congregation had been admonished from the pulpit not to ask for autographs and selfies. They fawned all over me though and made me feel special.

Avery desperately wanted to feel like a normal person when he was at home. Promotional tours, photo shoots, and fanfare didn't fit his personality, and he needed a break from them.

I'd not really seen that side of him. The Avery I knew was an actor. Once the cameras started rolling, he was a handsome, charismatic, outgoing, irresistible personality. At home, he was quiet and shy. Almost introverted.

I grew to love that about him.

It seemed like he opened up the most when he talked about his faith. He also talked a lot about his family, who I was nervous to meet. I shouldn't have been. They welcomed me immediately. Four sisters and two brothers. All married with kids. Avery was the youngest. They almost seemed relieved that he finally had a girlfriend. Especially his mother.

I adored them and it seemed like they liked me as well.

From Michigan, I went back to New York for a few days, then met Avery in Philadelphia so he could meet my much-smaller family consisting of my parents and one sister, still single. He was much more outgoing with them. Almost in the same way he played the part of a doting boyfriend in a movie. Not that it wasn't genuine, but he was determined to win over my family and did.

We grew closer by the minute. A familiarity developed between us as we got to know each other better. When we weren't together, we had long talks on the phone. One night, I opened up about Chris and told him everything. Avery listened intently and was extremely sympathetic and supportive.

But those conversations triggered a fear in me.

What if?

The waves of emotions shattered the euphoria of love that had set in and taken root.

By the end of the conversation, I didn't think I could marry Avery. What if he died? I couldn't go through that pain again. I'd never want to let him out of my sight.

So, I backed off. Became more distant. Guarded my heart. I think he noticed.

Thankfully, I had an excuse. I had to prepare for the rehearsals. I'd need hours of alone time to learn my lines. Avery wanted to learn them together, but I made up an excuse and told him I couldn't make a second trip to Nashville. Told him I learned better by myself.

When I finally did look at the script, another shocker emerged. I called Avery immediately.

"You're a country western singer in the movie," I said.

"Yep."

"In one of the scenes you sing me a song on a guitar."

"That's right. I've been practicing."

"Do you know how to play the guitar?"

"Yep."

"And you sing?"

"Don't be so surprised."

"Why didn't you say something?"

He didn't respond.

"I want you to sing to me. Over the phone. Right now. Put me on facetime so I can see you."

"On the piano or the guitar?"

"You play the piano?"

He had a piano in his house, but I thought it was for decoration. I couldn't believe it when he sat down and played a song by ear. And sang it beautifully. Then went to his room and retrieved a guitar. Played a different song. In a few notes, he skillfully pulled my heart back over the waterfall and into the river of love I felt for him.

"So, you're a triple threat," I said.

An entertainment term which meant he could act, sing, and dance.

"Oh no," he said. "I can't dance worth a flip. *Love Only* paid for dance lessons. I was so bad, they decided not to cast me in any movies where I had to dance."

"I can act and dance, but I can't sing."

"That's why God brought us together," he said. "We complete each other."

"You think God brought us together?"

"I do."

The thought warmed my heart. I could hardly believe God had blessed me again with such a wonderful person.

The fears were still there, but I was hooked again.

18

Three days before start of rehearsals

Rose finally had enough money to go on a shopping spree. Thanks to Noel Day and her three-movie deal with *Love Only*. The commissions in her last check equaled how much she earned all of last year.

Based on the success of the first two movies, Noel was the biggest star she had managed by far and had moved into the top ten overall in the agency based on her earning potential.

Love Only loved Noel, and Char negotiated a new, five-movie deal. Three more movies guaranteed with an option for two more. At a substantial raise. Noel would be getting more than five-hundred-thousand dollars per movie. Not as high as some of the women on the network but getting closer.

Another shopping spree was in the works once Rose started receiving royalties from that deal. She slipped off her Jimmy Choo pink pumps and set them by her chair. Something she'd seen her mom do a thousand times. Now she knew why she did it. It gave her a sense of importance. More than anything, Rose felt a sense of relief that she had finally won her mom's appreciation. As precarious as it might be.

She picked up the phone to call Noel and give her the good news about the new movie deal. Noel answered on the first ring.

"Hello, dear," Rose said, immediately regretting the tone which sounded like her mother whom she had vowed to never imitate.

"Rose," Noel said. "How are you?"

"I'm well. Are you excited to begin rehearsals on movie number three?"

The promotional tour was over, and rehearsals were scheduled to start next week. Filming right after.

"I am. I've been busy learning my lines."

"I have good news for you," Rose said. Something else her mother usually said to the client when she called to deliver the news of a new deal.

"I've been anticipating this call," Noel said.

Her tone seemed strange to Rose.

"Yes. *Love Only*—"

"I'm not doing any more *Love Only* movies," Noel interrupted.

Rose's heart took a tumble across the room. She couldn't believe what she'd just heard.

"What do you mean? My mom negotiated a new five-movie deal for you. With a substantial raise."

"Avery and I talked about it, and I'm not doing any more of them."

Rose tried to keep her tone from becoming confrontational. "That's crazy. They love you. You can write your own ticket. Do you know how many people would give their right arms to be in your situation?"

"I know and I appreciate all your work. But the decision is final."

"Why? Make me understand why you would turn down more than two-million dollars. Almost three million."

"I have other plans."

Anger rose to the surface like boiling lava in a volcano. Was it because of Avery? Watching them interact on the promotional tour convinced her they were dating. Was it more serious than that?

Avery was a multi-millionaire. Did Noel think she no longer needed the money? What if they broke up? Was she really willing to give up her career for him?

She'd try a different argument first.

"Noel, you're under contract with us. You have to take the deal."

"Our contract was up over a month ago. We never renewed it."

Panic shot through Rose like a high-speed sailboat through the wind. Sending her emotions spinning out of control without a rudder to steady them. All new clients were signed to a one-year contract. The agency had the right to renew it for an additional year.

Has it been a year?

Had she dropped the ball and not sent a renewal? If she remembered right, the contract stated that an intent to renew had to be sent within thirty days of the contract expiring.

"Hang on a minute," Rose said.

She looked in her drawer, and her heart sank to the bottom of her chest when she scanned the contract and realized Noel was right. It had expired more than thirty days ago. The ramifications of that fact hit her squarely in the head like a brick dropped from the Empire State Building.

Noel wasn't obligated to the *Love Only* deal. Technically, they shouldn't have even been negotiating on her behalf.

My mom is going to kill me!

"Can we at least discuss it? Can you come into the office? Or I'll come to you. You name it."

"I was going to suggest the same thing. How about two o'clock today at your office?"

It didn't matter if anything was on her schedule. Nothing was more important than this.

"I'll see you then," she said.

Rose hung up the phone slowly. Trying to process what this might mean. It meant her career had just been derailed. Crashed and burned might be more descriptive. Her mom would never trust her with another client again.

How could I have been so stupid?

She picked up the phone and dialed her mom's extension.

"Are you available?" she asked.

As much as she dreaded having to tell her the news, she had to get it over with as fast as possible. Like ripping off a bandage. More like pulling the stitches out yourself. Before the wound had healed.

"Sure. Come on."

Her mom sounded in a good mood. *Not for long.*

The walk to the office felt like a death march.

She sat behind her mom's see-through glass custom Italian-made desk with her red Louboutin spiked heels sitting on the floor beside her. The smile on her face only made things worse.

Rose slumped into the chair and groaned.

"What's wrong?" Char asked.

"I spoke to Noel."

"What is it this time?"

Her mom had mentioned on more than one occasion how difficult Noel was sometimes. Not that she meant to be. But with the slap at the audition and the debacle at the restaurant, they'd had their share of drama with her. At least she wasn't doing drugs, getting arrested, or releasing a sex tape. Although, ironically enough, in today's environment, those things often helped a career.

"I told Noel about the *Love Only* movie deal. She doesn't want to do it."

"She has no choice. Tell her to read her contract."

"That's the problem. She's no longer under contract." Rose moaned again.

"What do you mean she's not under contract?" Char exploded.

"It expired a month ago."

"This is unbelievable! We have the right to an automatic renewal. How did you let this happen?"

"I don't know. I screwed up. I didn't realize a year had passed."

"That's why you put it in your calendar. This is basic 101 paying attention to details. Something you've never been good at. Do you know what this means? You've cost this firm tens of thousands of dollars."

"I know. It's my fault."

"It sure is! You have no one to blame but yourself. I can't believe you."

"She's coming in this afternoon. I'm going to try to fix this."

"I want to be there."

"It's at two."

"I can't be there," Mom said with exasperation. "I'm meeting with Art Kingston at two. I can't change it."

Art Kingston was our biggest client. Almost as big as Avery Johnson in the world of entertainment management.

"I'll meet with her. I can get things back on track."

"Why doesn't she want to do the *Love Only* movies?" Before Rose could answer, Char's mouth flew open. "She's going to Avery's agent. That's the only thing that makes sense. If they're an item now, he's convinced her to leave us in the dust."

"I didn't think of that."

"Who is his agent? I want to call them and tell them they can't steal my client. I found that girl. I made her a star."

"I don't know who his agent is."

Char picked up the phone and called her assistant on the speakerphone. "Find out who represents Avery Johnson."

"We don't know," her assistant said. "You asked me to dig around a couple years ago. That information is a secret."

Char tapped her fingers rapidly on the desk.

"Somebody has to know. Keep digging. I'll make some phone calls." She roughly cut off the call.

"You ..." Char said, pointing at Rose, "get out of my sight. I don't want to see your face at the moment. I'll deal with you later."

"I can fix this."

"You'd better."

Rose slinked out of the office like a wounded duck. *What if I can't fix it?*

19

@Two o'clock couldn't come fast enough although in some ways, it came too fast. Rose didn't remember ever dreading anything as much as she feared that meeting.

What would her mother do if she lost Noel as a client forever? Firing her would be the best outcome she could hope for in that situation. Staying on having her mother constantly reminding her of how big a failure she was would be way worse.

How did this happen? She'd finally gotten a star to manage, and she'd blown it. Perhaps her mom was right. She wasn't cut out for this business.

The receptionist called and said, "Your two o'clock appointment is here." Finally putting her out of her waiting misery.

"Thank you."

"I'll send them in."

"Them?"

"Yes. Mr. Johnson is here as well."

Her already queasy stomach churned harder. Of course, he came with her. To make sure they didn't give her any trouble.

The couple appeared at the door of her office within seconds. Noel was beaming. Avery was looking handsome and happy as well.

Rose greeted them warmly although she felt like a girlfriend about to be dumped by her boyfriend of one year. The boyfriend she thought was the one.

"You look great," Noel said, in the friendliest of tones. "I love your shoes."

Rose wondered if she should return them and get her money back. She probably couldn't since she'd worn them several times.

"You look like a million bucks yourself," Rose said. She noticed that Noel and Avery both were clearly in love. They weren't even trying to hide it.

It reminded Rose that not only was her career in the toilet, but she was older than Noel with no prospects of an engagement soon. She didn't even have a boyfriend. As if she needed that thought to pop into her mind.

"Please, have a seat," Rose said as she closed the door behind them.

She walked around to her desk and sat forward with her elbows on the desk. Something that made her look anxious, but she didn't care. She was anxious.

"We don't want to lose you as a client," Rose said, skipping the pleasantries.

Noel twisted her lips to the side.

"Why would you lose me as a client? I love working with you."

Rose refused to let her spirit soar. Not until she understood what was going on.

"I thought … I mean … Based on our last conversation, I thought maybe you were leaving us. That maybe you wanted another agent. Mom thought you might be switching to Avery's agent."

Noel waved her hand dismissively.

"I'm sorry I left you with that impression. I didn't mean to."

What was I supposed to think?

"I don't want to do any more *Love Only* movies after this one, but that doesn't mean I'm leaving the agency. You've been so good to me."

"O ... kay. So, what do you want to do? Those *Love Only* movies are your meal ticket. Mom negotiated a good deal for you."

Noel and Avery were holding hands. They did look perfect for each other.

"That's why we wanted to meet with you," Avery interjected. "I've been offered a role in a major motion picture with one of the big studios."

"Congratulations."

"Big budget film. They want Noel to star in it with me."

Rose could no longer hold back the elation.

"And you want us to represent Noel's interest?" she said excitedly.

"We want you to represent both of us."

Rose was sitting back in her chair when Avery spoke those words and almost went sprawling backward. She quickly sat forward again when she regained her balance.

"You want us to represent both of you," she said, as if she didn't believe it. Which she didn't.

"Yes," Noel answered. "I told Avery how much I love you and how good a job you do for me. You also said you need a big star to get your mother's attention."

Noel winked at her. She placed her hand palm up and toward Avery.

"Voila. Is Avery big enough for ya?"

"Of course. I mean ... I'd love to represent you. Are you sure you want me and not my mother?"

Obviously, her mother would be involved. She'd have to draw up the contracts and be involved in the negotiations. Even if they wanted her, surely her mom would want to have Avery under her control.

"We want you, silly," Noel said. "That's why we're here talking to you and not to your mother."

"It makes sense for you to represent both of us," Avery said. "Keep it all in the family."

"Who has been representing you, Avery? Are you out of contract? Ethically, I can't pursue you as a client if you have a contract with someone else."

"I represent myself. Always have."

"Oh."

That's why her mom couldn't find out who represented him.

"The negotiations are going to be complex. We want to be executive producers on the film. We also want royalty rights with a piece of the profits moving forward along with a large upfront fee."

"We can do that."

"They've thrown out some figures. Twenty-million dollars for me. Five for Noel. I think we can do better, but I don't think I'm equipped to cover all the bases. That's why we want you and your firm to negotiate the deal."

Rose's jaw would've dropped to the floor had it not been connected to her neck. The most her mom ever got Art Kingston was eight million.

"Like I said, I'd be honored to represent you. What about your *Love Only* deal? Are you under contract with them? Does it preclude you from taking other roles?"

It must not or he wouldn't be here. Why am I creating my own objections? Close the deal my mother would say.

Avery said, "My deal with them is movie to movie. Always has been. I never wanted to tie myself into a long-term deal."

"Hang on a minute," Rose said, as she stood to her feet. "Wait here. I'd like to get my mom and tell her the good news."

"We'll find something to do," Noel said, like a giddy schoolgirl. She looked so happy.

She couldn't possibly be as happy as I am.

Her mom was going to freak out.

Rose practically sprinted to her office. The assistant was at her desk.

"I need to talk to mom."

"She's with Mr. Kingston and is not to be disturbed."

"I think she will want to be disturbed. Tell her I need to talk to her."

The assistant was reluctant.

"Don't worry. Trust me. She'll be fine with it."

The assistant picked up the handset and dialed the number. Rose could hear her mother's annoyed voice on the other end, obviously wondering why her meeting was being interrupted.

"Your daughter needs to see you. She said it's important."

The door opened a few seconds later and Char stomped out with a clear look of disbelief that Rose had the audacity to bother her when she was meeting with the firm's most important client.

Little did she know that the most important client was now sitting in Rose's office.

"What is it?"

"I'm meeting with Noel."

"And? Did you save her as a client?"

"Yes," Rose said smugly.

"Well, that's a relief. Fill me in on the details later."

She turned and put her hand on the doorknob and started to go back into her office.

"There's more," Rose said.

She turned back around and furrowed her brow like she really wasn't happy with Rose. "Hurry up and get to the point. Art is waiting."

"Avery Johnson's in my office," Rose said.

Char's left eyebrow raised halfway up her forehead.

"He wants *me* to represent him as well."

The other eyebrow raced up her forehead as well.

Rose tried to maintain a serious and businesslike manner. She spoke calmly and succinctly. Really, she wanted to shout the words. Then go to the top of the building and scream them at the top of her lungs.

"You're kidding."

"Nope. He's got a big box office deal he wants us to negotiate for him. He said they've already offered him twenty million."

Char abruptly opened the door to her office and stuck her head inside.

"Art, I'll be a few minutes," she said. "Make yourself comfortable. Can I get you anything?"

She closed the door and started walking with a purpose toward Rose's office. Muttering to herself, but loud enough for Rose to hear her.

"You might become my favorite daughter yet," she said.

"I'm your only daughter!"

Char stopped in her tracks and turned around. She took Rose's arm and walked with her together. Like Rose was her equal.

"I never doubted you for a minute," she said.

So, this is what my mother's approval feels like.

I need to enjoy it while it lasts.

20

The fear had returned like an avalanche.

I couldn't do it.

I didn't have the strength.

I didn't think I could survive another loss.

I would have to end things with Avery before they went too far. I'd already let them go too far. He was head over heels in love with me and I had led him on. I was hopelessly in love with him as well, but it had to be done.

I had to wait until we finished the movie.

When filming started, the love for Avery overwhelmed me. So I wouldn't be distracted, I threw myself into the role and put breaking up with him on the back burner. Which wasn't easy since my character was attracted to him and would eventually fall in love and get engaged.

Ugh! Engaged.

I felt uncomfortable. It took all my will to put the fears out of my mind and allow myself to fall in love all over again with Chase, my love interest in the movie. I had a hard time separating him from Avery.

We filmed in Canada, so we'd have an abundance of snow. The story was set at Christmas. My character, Brooke, was a first-grade, special-ed teacher in a small town called New Hope.

Brooke and Chase dated all through high school and were even engaged in college. After graduation, Brooke took the job as teacher, and

Chase worked on his music. When he was suddenly discovered by a music producer and offered a record deal, he had to move to Nashville. He tried to get Brooke to go with him.

She couldn't leave her kids she loved so much. He couldn't turn down the record deal, so they broke off their engagement in an emotional goodbye scene.

It felt too real. This was what it'd be like when I had to break up with Avery.

A real tearjerker. I already felt the pain of losing Avery so acting out the scenes felt natural to me.

In the movie, Chase came back to town for Christmas. It's like he never left. Brooke still loved him, and he wasn't over her. But the issues remained. She loved her job and her kids. He was a big star with obligations. After the Christmas holidays, he was set to go on tour for six months.

A typical romance trope. Impossible love.

That's what I had with Avery. It could never work. When he left to film a movie, I could see myself constantly stressed. Wondering if he'd make it back to me. Doing this movie brought back the emotions of losing Chris.

The filming took twenty-one weeks, which only prolonged my anxiety. Avery played the part of Chase brilliantly. Sang the songs himself live with a band which was why it took longer to film.

In the last scene, Chase had to leave to go on tour. In the days before, Brooke had pulled away, unable to deal with the emotions of losing him all over again. I knew how that felt, because I felt it myself. My heart was already broken even though I hadn't lost Avery yet.

In the movie, Chase wanted to say goodbye, but Brooke refused to meet him to see him off, so he went to her house. She didn't open the door and pretended she wasn't home. Too painful to deal with.

It brought back memories of me pounding on Avery's hotel room door. Demanding an explanation. He gave me one. He deserved as much from me.

Could I find the words? Would he understand why we couldn't be together? I wished there was a way to break up with him without actually having to do it.

When Brooke didn't answer the door to her house, Chase was supposed to walk back to his van and drive off into the sunset. Before he does, Brooke bursts out the door and runs after him. She throws her arms around him and kisses him. Intending to only say goodbye, so they wouldn't leave the relationship on such bad terms.

Instead, after the passionate kiss, Chase gets down on one knee, pulls out a ring, and puts it on Brooke's finger.

"Will you marry me for real this time?" he asks.

Brooke recoils in fear and says, "You know I can't. It won't work. It'll never work."

"We'll figure it out."

"I can't. I don't want to go through the pain of saying goodbye to you over and over again. I need a husband who's here with me. All the time."

Brooke took off the ring and accidentally dropped it in the snow. There's a frantic search for it. A humorous scene designed to break the tension for the viewer.

Eventually, Brooke finds it and puts the ring back on her finger, to the surprise of Chase.

"Does this mean you'll marry me?" he asks.

"I'll never take it off. You're right. Love will win in the end."

They kiss. That doesn't change the fact that Chase has to go. After a tearful goodbye, he gets in the van and drives away. The movie ends when Brooke walks out on the road and watches him. She waves as tears stream down her face. She clutches her hand and the ring on her finger as he slowly goes out of view.

Why did this feel so much like real life?

21

The time came to film the scene. The director went over a few last-minute instructions. Real snow fell which added to the ambiance but created more complications. The lenses had to be kept dry and we were cold. The sidewalk was also slippery, so I had to be careful when I ran out of the house.

The director wanted us to film the entire scene without breaks. To capture the entire moment in real time. Which put more pressure on us. Often shooting scenes was nothing more than one shot, a change of position, then we filmed another one. In some instances, we could shoot an entire scene, including dialogue, and the other person didn't need to be there. If it didn't call for us to be in the camera at the same time, we just pretended we were talking to each other.

"Let's get this in one take," I said to Avery, before I had to go inside the house.

"I'll get my part right," Avery said. "If one of us messes up, the other has to buy dinner."

"Deal."

Although I dreaded the thought of it. Would I really have the courage to break up with him at dinner? That was my plan, but I didn't know if I could follow through with it.

I couldn't think about it now. I got into position inside the house and mentally went through the scene in my mind.

The director must've said action because Avery, Chase, pounded on the door. After a few seconds of knocking, he abruptly turned and walked down the steps toward his van. At the assistant director's cue, I burst out of the house and down the stairs, careful not to fall on the slick snow.

I jumped into his arms, and we kissed passionately.

"I'll miss you," I said. The line wasn't in the script but seemed appropriate. The director didn't stop us, so we continued.

I meant it. I would miss Avery desperately.

Chase got down on one knee. Reached into his pocket and pulled out the ring.

I gasped and put my hands to my mouth. He took my hand and pulled it toward him. He carefully placed the ring on my finger. We'd rehearsed it a dozen times.

My hand shook from the cold which worked well for the tension in the scene.

"Noel, will you marry me for real this time?" he asked.

I pulled away, as the script called for me to do.

"You know I can't. It won't work. It'll never work."

I took the ring off my finger and dropped it in the snow.

"What did you do that for?" Avery said and started to frantically look for it.

That's not the line.

You owe me dinner.

Wait.

Did he say Noel or Brooke?

I vaguely remember he said *my* name. I must've imagined it. He obviously said Brooke. The director hadn't yelled cut.

"I can't find the ring," Avery said, with panic behind the words. "That ring cost a fortune."

The ring was fake. It looked good on the camera but wasn't worth a dollar in a garage sale.

"Help me look."

We finally found it and Avery was relieved. We stood to our feet. I looked at the ring. It wasn't the one we used during rehearsals. It looked real.

It suddenly dawned on me what was happening.

"Do you really want me to marry you?" I said, as I looked deep into his eyes for the truth.

"Yes."

He's serious. He's asking me to marry him. For real.

"But I'm afraid. What if?"

He put his finger on my lips.

"We'll make it work."

"Do you promise?"

"I promise."

Before I could stop myself, I said, "Absolutely yes! I will marry you."

A huge smile came on his face. He put the ring back on my finger. We kissed again. I don't know for how long.

"This really is a Christmas to remember," Avery said, when our lips parted.

"And ... cut! That's a wrap," the director shouted.

Even though I was freezing, my whole body felt warm and tingly.

"What does this mean?" I turned and asked Avery.

"It means we're engaged."

"For real?"

"Yes."

"I thought you were acting."

"I wasn't."

The director was beside Avery now.

"Were you in on this?" I asked. His sly grin confirmed what I suspected.

"Don't we need to shoot it again?" Avery asked.

"We're done. I don't think you can improve on the real thing."

"But I said Noel, not Brooke."

"We'll dub over it. Everything was perfect. You were terrific, Noel. You seemed genuinely surprised."

"I'm speechless."

"I wish the two of you all the happiness in the world." He stepped back and motioned for us to face the crowd.

A large number of people had gathered at the set. The entire throng erupted in loud cheers and applause.

The fears were still there, but it didn't matter.

I savored the moment.

I'm engaged!

Rose and Erin Palmer were quickly by our side. I could tell they were in on it as well.

"We've been talking," Erin said. "*Love Only* would like to televise your wedding live."

"You're kidding," I said.

"We never kid about money," Rose said. "The ratings will be huge."

I looked at Avery. He shrugged.

"Sounds like a good idea to me," he said. "Everybody else is doing it, why shouldn't we?"

"Okay," I said, feeling completely overwhelmed.

This all seemed too good to be true.

I looked up in the sky. Snow tickled my nose.

I said a prayer and thanked God. Even thanked Chris for understanding. He'd want me to be happy. I was sure of it.

Thank you for purchasing this novel from best-selling author, Terry Toler. As an additional thank you, Terry wants to give you a free gift.

Sign up for:

Updates
New Releases
Announcements

At terrytoler.com

We'll send you an eBook, *The Book Club*, a Cliff Hangers novella, free of charge.

READ MORE BOOKS FROM TERRY TOLER

Jamie Austen Thrillers

Read all the Jamie Austen Thrillers. They must be good. They've been number one on Amazon in ten different countries. Click on the link below.

THE JAMIE AUSTEN THRILLERS (12 book series)
Kindle Edition (amazon.com)

https://amzn.to/3vmPUy7

Cliff Hangers Mystery Series

Who wants to read a good mystery? We've got you covered! Read the Cliff Hangers where homicide detective, Cliff Ford, solves crimes in Chicago, with help from his wife Julia. These books have everything Terry Toler is known for. Page turning suspense, a hint of romance, and an ending you won't see coming.

The Cliff Hangers Mystery Series (4 book series)
Kindle Edition (amazon.com)

https://www.amazon.com/gp/product/B09GKY2KH1

About Terry

Terry Toler is an Amazon international # 1 best-selling and award-winning author. He writes clean fiction with a message and life-changing nonfiction. He's a public speaker, entrepreneur, and has authored more than forty books.

Sign up for his newsletter where you'll get free stuff, exclusive content, and news of releases and promotions. He can be followed at terrytoler.com.

If you like his books, please take a few minutes to leave a review on Amazon. We really appreciate it. It helps draw more readers to his books. Thanks!